Reading Borough Libraries

Email: info@readinglibraries.org.uk
Website: www.readinglibraries.org.uk

Reading   0118 901

D1757592

WH₁ 07/06   08 JUL 08   THE ...... BAT . 1.2

05. OCT ..

17 ....

Reading Borough Council

34126001351736

BUZZARD'S BREED

When Jim Storme went to join his brother Red, and his cousin, Bart McGivern, in Wyoming, he was heading for trouble. Cattle barons were attacking lesser men, and branding them as rustlers . . . Jim joined the cattlemen's mercenaries, but he changed sides when confronted by his brother, Red. When a wagon loaded with dynamite hit their ranch, it was one of many clashes between settlers and invaders in which the three Texans made their mark, and struggled to survive.

Books by David Bingley
in the Linford Western Library:

THE BEAUCLERC BRAND
ROGUE'S REMITTANCE
STOLEN STAR
BRIGAND'S BOUNTY
TROUBLESHOOTER ON TRIAL
GREENHORN GORGE
RUSTLERS' MOON
SUNSET SHOWDOWN
TENDERFOOT TRAIL BOSS
HANGTOWN HEIRESS
HELLIONS' HIDEAWAY
THE JUDGE'S TERRITORY
KILLERS' CANYON
SIX-SHOOTER JUNCTION
THE DIAMOND KID
RED ROCK RENEGADES
HELLIONS AT LARGE

DAVID BINGLEY

BUZZARD'S BREED

Complete and Unabridged

LINFORD
Leicester

First published in Great Britain in 1967

First Linford Edition
published 2006

British Library CIP Data

Bingley, David
    Buzzard's breed.—Large print ed.—
Linford western library
1. Western stories
2. Large type books
I. Title
823.9'14 [F]

ISBN 1–84617–354–X

Published by
F. A. Thorpe (Publishing)
Anstey, Leicestershire

Set by Words & Graphics Ltd.
Anstey, Leicestershire
Printed and bound in Great Britain by
T. J. International Ltd., Padstow, Cornwall

This book is printed on acid-free paper

1

There were many saloons in the Western states with the colourful name of the 'Golden Eagle'. The one in Albion Creek, Idaho, near the border with Wyoming, was not a whole lot different from many another of its kind. It had a long bar running along the rear of the main room, a pot-bellied stove in a dark corner, and two types of tables seemingly scattered almost haphazardly across the sanded floor.

The tables with the green baize tops were to the right, and there was more lamplight over them. The men whose heads were tilted down over the soiled pasteboard cards had less to say than the men whose primary interest was in drinking. The eight card players were all using hard liquor. One group of four consisted of all local men.

The other four looked ill-assorted.

Three of them were seasonal waddies, who had just been paid off, and the other man — the one with the short fair hair and slightly Roman nose — also had the itch to move on to new parts and a different job.

Jim Storme, for that was his name, had had a lease on a part of a silver mine for exactly eighteen months. He had realised on the silver which he had extracted, and when he had bought himself a fine dun horse and the wherewithal to move his tall, muscular Texas frame to other parts, he found that he had little more than two hundred dollars in hand to show for his labours.

Now, he was risking his hard-earned dollars in a game of chance, and his mind was not as firmly fixed on the game as it should have been, if he was to add to his pile.

Jim had finished his business in town earlier that day. He had deliberated for a long time before deciding to risk his money at the card table, and when he had come to a decision, he had purchased six small cigars to help him with his concentration. No one around the card playing area could have failed to see the distant look in his keen green eyes. Here was a man who could be skinned, if it could be done without bringing him back to the present too soon.

From time to time, the men playing with him peered into the lean face with the pointed chin, which was partially hidden in shadow under the distinctive dun stetson. The hat's brim was rolled to a point at the front in such a way as to throw a triangular shadow down the face, making it seem even thinner and longer than it was.

The snake band around the hat was the only unusual adornment in Jim's outfit. His shirt was of a pale scrubbed blue. His denims were worn, but clean. There was little about him to categorise him for the others.

His rivals in the game were Sim Roberts, Jack Darnell and Lon West.

They had been playing for a little over two hours when Jack Darnell won for the first time and collected from the others. He made little of his victory, in case Storme came to his senses and made the game all that much harder to win. Roberts, a man with a fattening waistline and thinning hair, was the type who only lost his roll slowly. Lon West, the third man, was the one who finally expected to scoop all available funds. He was a broad-faced, beady-eyed, cunning player who had already added half Jim's money to his own pile.

West watched the way in which Darnell's black moustache pivoted on his short upper lip, and sent him a glance which warned him not to make too much of his recent winnings. Jim merely nodded and rocked easily on his chair. He yawned, refilled his shot glass from the communal bottle, and lit another cigar from the one which was burned down.

He had done more thinking about his past, present and future in the last twenty-four hours than he had done in the whole of the eighteen months since he arrived in Idaho state.

*   *   *

Three tough young Texans had come north together from a town called Plainview in the southern part of the lone star state's Panhandle. Jim's brother, Red, was two years older, and at six feet in height, two inches taller. The Storme brothers, Jim and Red, had always got along with each other. They had been raised on the ranch of their uncle, Dan Pinson, on Diamond P range, and their physical strength and all-round skill at ranching pursuits had helped to make old Pinson wealthy.

Bart McGivern, a distant cousin, who was only slightly older than Red, had chosen to ride north with the Storme boys and seek his fortune, or at least a different way of life, in and around the infant state of Wyoming.

For the record, Red Storme's hair

was sandy-red rather than carroty-red. Cousin Bart's colouring was dark. He matched the Stormes for height, but weighed more, being thick and strong through the shoulders.

Inevitably, during the long trek from Texas to Wyoming, the three young men had become a little tired of each other's company. Fellow travellers going south had stopped to talk with them, and had helped them to make up their minds as to the kind of jobs they would take. Red had been very definite. He was fascinated with the idea of starting humbly in the cattle business and building up. He wanted to find a man with the right ideas and help him to build.

Bart had been passionately fond of people's rights. Helping a small rancher to become a big one would not necessarily give Bart the satisfaction that Red would derive from it, but when Jim put forward his suggestion of heading westward into Idaho to try his hand in a silver mine, Bart had sufficiently known his mind to say that he was staying in Wyoming with Red.

There had been a parting of the ways. Neither Red nor Bart had thought much of Jim's silver mining idea, and that had prompted Jim to stick in at his self-appointed task long after he knew that he would make little out of it.

And here he was, in the 'Golden Eagle', thinking back to that time of parting, a year and a half ago, and thinking that he might have been a whole lot happier if he had shelved his own idea and gone on to Jackson County with Red and Bart.

Sim Roberts yawned rather loudly, and was kicked under the table by West for his trouble. While the cards were dealt again, Roberts, Darnell and West searched each other's eyes, as though they could not believe their luck. Incredibly, Jim started playing, as before, although he had lost again with a good hand.

Jim's thoughts had taken him back to

the Plainview area of Texas, to the Pinsons' Diamond P, and the neighbouring Bar D outfit owned by the Dix family. The Bar D, in the old days, had twin attractions; namely, Maybell and her twin brother, Sam, who would inherit the ranch in years to come. Maybell had very long blonde hair and light blue eyes. She was shapely, and as strong as her brother. Of the three men who had ridden north, Jim had been the one who attracted her most. He had been attracted himself, but he never did quite figure out why she liked him more than Red and Bart. He thought, at times, that it was because he appreciated her prowess in the saddle, and with the lariat and six-gun.

Red and Bart, perhaps, tended to ignore the skills of which she was so proud, and tried to treat her exclusively as a woman.

★　★　★

A half-inch of cigar ash fell off the end of Jim's cigar and settled on his handful of cards. He blinked hard and frowned at the resultant mess, for the first time bringing the whole of his mind to the job in hand. He became aware that his fellow players were waiting for him. Their eyes, when he sought them, were keen and scrupulously patient.

He had an attack of conscience.

'Doggone it, boys, I must be a whole lot on the sentimental side, I must admit. All this time I've been thinkin' of this an' that, an' not givin' the best part of my mind to the game in hand. Here an' now I'm askin' you to forgive me. From here on in I'll try to make amends, so help me!'

Darnell and Roberts murmured mild approval. West, who had all of Jim's money barring fifty dollars, began to tense up. He was beginning to wonder if Jim had been playing them along all this time. He was not the sort of man who could shrug off such a matter, if his surmise turned out to be a correct one.

That game was a tense one. West had the best hand, but by a colossal piece of bluff, Jim won the game, and two men who had been idly standing by congratulated him rather heartily upon the change in his luck. The loner took back some of his money, and remarked on the earliness of the hour. It was barely six in the evening, and West knew that if things went against him and his buddies they would not be able to call a halt to the game for several hours.

He had visions of his waddy's pay dwindling game by game, because he knew better than most that he was only a passably good player, and one who could be beaten by a thinking man whose concentration was good.

Jim started to improvise on an old Texas lullaby with Spanish words. Some time later, he won again, and when Darnell's moustache twitched for the wrong sort of reason, the Texan called for a fresh bottle of liquor and more cigars. More watchers sided the game, and in the face of Jim's whipped-up enthusiasm, the men who were beginning to lose, had to play on.

Roberts played with his eyes squinted unhappily over his fat jowl and second chin. Darnell frequently explored the underside of his moustache with an elongated underlip. West fretted and fumed in a quiet sort of way, while the perspiration leaked out below the tightly-fitted and curly-brimmed hat which graced his rounded head.

Jim eased back into the shadow and played like he had done before, except that he flashed those perceptive green eyes from time to time and showed his teeth in a broad grin at the end of the games.

It was barely eight-thirty in the evening when Lon West gave in with a bad grace and went to join his buddies at the bar. Jim offered to shake him by the hand, but the offer was spurned. Instead, the Texan shrugged and bent to count and collect up his winnings. He was wondering whether he would tell Red and Bart about his winnings at the table when he caught up with them, or whether he would let them think he had made the extra cash in the mine.

Some ten yards away from him, Sim Roberts, who was well on the way to being drunk, complained: 'Well, hell an' tarnation, Lon, you know like Jack an' me that we couldn't afford to lose all that money to the Texan!'

The voice rose on a note of protest. Roberts was about to go on, but following a significant glance from West, Darnell thumped the talker hard in the small of the back, hurting him and temporarily depriving him of the power of speech.

Jim straightened up and noticed what had happened. He also took in West's glance of malevolent hatred, and for the first time since he made contact with the three waddies he began to entertain the idea that he might have trouble over his winnings.

He wondered how fast West was with the twin forty-fours which hung so low around his thighs.

★ ★ ★

An hour after sundown, Jim was regarding the fire in his night camp alongside of a shallow slow-running stream, east of Albion Creek.

If anyone was coming after him, they would have no difficulty in knowing the direction in which to look. Following the prolonged card game, he had talked with the barman and two local tradesmen in the saloon, and the proprietor of an eating house further down the street.

He had made no attempt to hide his future movements. Everyone in town knew that the quiet young Texan who had worked the Roxy Silver Mine was headed for the Wyoming border in an effort to trace his kin. He could have put his mount aboard a train going in the right direction the following day, but as he was a little out of practice at saddle work, he had decided against such a move.

As he pushed his hat further over his forehead, he reflected that the train might have been a whole lot safer than lone trail-riding such as he had elected to do.

The dun horse, pegged out some ten yards away, showed slight unrest. Jim stopped admiring its silhouette and decided that it had heard something which it did not approve of. Under the blanket, he had with him his Winchester and .45 Colt. He began to think he might have to use one or the other of them before the night was out.

He took off his hat and stuck it up on his saddle in such a way as to make it appear that he was still under the blanket. His roll had to be altered a bit, but when he left it and crawled towards the water he felt that a man whose eyes were teased with darkness might think he was still in the roll and sleeping.

Bootless, he crept into the stream

and walked a little to the north of the depression where the fire was and the nervous horse.

He covered fifty yards with the coolness of the water gradually making itself felt up to his thighs. A branch of a small willow plucked at his denims and he decided that he had gone far enough. He used the willow to haul himself out of the water. Without undue loss of time, he stripped off his wet denims and replaced them with a dry pair which he had taken along for the purpose.

The dun began to flick its black mane and tail, and to pace through half circles at the full extent of its tether. It whinneyed quietly and once it turned to look in the direction which its master had gone. The would-be killer was careful in his approach. Only two small sounds carried to Jim's straining ears in the half-hour after he had shifted his position.

One was caused by a snapping twig, and the other was the sound of a displaced stone. The Texan intended to let the attack develop to the full. He would watch and thus be informed as to the number of his enemies, and the ruthlessness with which they would attack.

No other sound came to suggest that the first crawling man had company. The intruder moved to within twenty yards before rising silently to his feet with a revolver in each fist. Jim could not see his face, but he could imagine the expression when both guns were cocked and six bullets were discharged into the blanket and bed roll.

The night gear kicked and writhed under the flying lead. It was only just still again when Jim swallowed hard.

'West, is that you?'

Although he had only whispered, his voice sounded loud in the comparative quiet after the gun explosions. West uttered a hoarse cry from his throat and sprang to face what he now knew to be a redoubtable menace. He fired off three more shots, some of which went close, before Jim decided on his fate.

The steady Winchester emitted two bullets with a short interval between. Both of the leaden missiles found a place in the killer's heart, though he failed to fall to the earth for another fifteen seconds. When he dropped he went down heavily. Jim came a little closer, and murmured things to help the dun to calm down. He then made a slight detour to take him back in the direction from which West had crawled.

Everything was quiet. He yawned and decided against searching at dark for the other man's horse. He walked back to the corpse, which was grimacing, even in death, and dragged West towards the fire. There, he left him, while he returned to his previous lookout spot under a fallen log.

In spite of the uncertainty in the isolated area, the Texan was asleep within five minutes of laying down his head.

2

The moon gave way to the sun in front of Lon West's unwinking eyes. Jim removed the hat and threw it over the ugly face without undue concern. He went about the business of boosting the fire and making breakfast prompted by a healthy emptiness in his stomach.

He ate and drank standing up, and while he fed the inner man he wondered what was the best thing to do with West. In the past eighteen months he had done a whole lot of digging and scraping, and the idea of digging a grave for his would-be killer did not please him.

Again, he was slow to make up his mind, but when he was sure, he felt cheered. He would backtrack into Albion Creek and take West's remains with him. As likely as not Darnell and Roberts would be sleeping off the liquor of the night before. They could see to his burial, and perhaps be a few dollars in hand after they had sold his horse.

The animal in question was a sinewy buckskin with a holdfast sore on its left foreleg.

★   ★   ★

A little after ten in the morning, Jim gave the barest details of what had occurred to the Town Marshal and allowed him to examine Lon West's mortal remains. There was little to discuss, and no need for any cross-examination. Any townsman could read the story for himself.

West had taken his licking at cards in the worst possible spirit. He had followed the man who had won his money out of town with the express intention of killing him to get the money back again. His own ruthlessness had brought about his death. Side by side on the sidewalk, Jim and the Marshal examined the unsightly remains. The peace officer turned to Jim with an unspoken question framing his features.

'Are those other two waddies, Darnell an' Roberts, still in town?' Jim queried, speaking first.

'Well, so far as I know they are, Jim,' the Marshal opined. 'Ain't seen nothin' of them since the saloon closed last night, an' they ain't the energetic types. I reckon you'll find them some place or another sleepin' themselves sober. Are you figurin' on turnin' this jasper over to them?'

Jim nodded. He explained what he had in mind, and at once received the peace officer's approval. He took the two horses down the street and kept them moving until he found the two men in question curled up on a bench outside a cheap eating house.

Something made Jim tip over the bench, so that the sleepers fell heavily to the boards and awoke. They looked him over and forgot their angry words. Without looking too closely, they knew who the stiff would be on the back of the buckskin. Their eyes could not meet Jim's as he explained what he thought of their partner, and of them.

He went on: 'If you go along to the big livery you might be able to sell his hoss. The price it fetches could cover a burial, an' have a little left over. An' while you're at the livery, you could take in my hoss an' have the fellow there give it some attention. Tell him I'll be along there in a few hours.'

The two crestfallen men fought for the honour of leading the dun. Jack Darnell won, but he got no thanks for his efforts. Jim was already regarding the vacated bench with covetous eyes. Before the discomfited men were properly out of sight, he had curled up on the bench and tipped his hat over his eyes.

★ ★ ★

The sound of chuckles coming from the throat of a man with a rich and fruity voice brought Jim out of sleep two hours later.

'Well doggone me, I suppose everythin' they're sayin' about you, young fellow, is true.'

Jim peered up from under his hat brim, and beheld the well-rounded neatly dressed figure of Vic Conners, one of the local cattlemen. Conners was fifty-five years of age. He was sunburnt, bald, and slightly paunched, but his clothing, topped by a cream stetson made him a commanding figure.

Jim cleared his throat. 'If you're lookin' for hands, Mister Conners, you're fresh out of luck. Although I came back to town, I still intend to ride into Wyomin' an' look up my brother an' cousin. So — '

'Now see here, young fellow, I'm seekin' to do you a favour, in a way. How would you like to travel to the other side of Wyomin' state in the quickest an' most comfortable fashion, eh?'

Jim sat up. 'If you mean by rail, I've considered that an' decided I was a little short on hoss ridin' practice. But I appreciate your interest, jest the same.'

Conners was not to be put off. 'I want you to go by train an' be met at the other end by the agent of some associates of mine. They're short of good cowhands, and they'd pay your expenses for the journey to join them, if you'd only say the word.'

The eating house at Jim's back was reminding him that several hours had elapsed since breakfast. Conners observed this. His smile broadened.

'There's a train goin' east at one o'clock. Plenty of time to get outside a good meal an' wind up your affairs. Couldn't find a better way of travellin', no siree! Now, why don't you give it a try? My associates at the other end won't hold it against you if you change your mind. Besides, it might take you a while to locate your kin, seein' as how you ain't seen them for a year or more. Do you have letters?'

Jim shook his head about the letters, and checked on when the locomotive would be leaving. He entered the eating house and gave the matter some more thought. When he came out, he hurried to the livery, brought out his dun and paid the bill. He was at the rail depot ten minutes before the woodburner rolled in alongside the platform.

Vic Conners spotted him early on. He pushed a furlough ticket into his hands and introduced him to the conductor as soon as that worthy had his foot on the platform. The official showed grudging interest, and took Jim along to the horse box, while Conners kept pace with them and fired off reasons he thought would encourage Jim to take up with the Wyoming ranchers.

Jim thought, as he ran the horse into the box, that it might be amusing if Red's boss came to meet him and to offer him a job in the new state, but something about Conners' anxiety to get him on the way to Wyoming damped his enthusiasm down. When he was in the carriage, Jim stuck his head out of the window.

'Where was it you said this agent would locate me, Mister Conners?'

'Either in Laramie or Cheyenne, Jim! Whichever place he's in, the agent will find you. Take it easy, an' don't have any qualms about bein' met!' As an afterthought, he added: 'I sure do hope you'll find your kin without too much difficulty!'

Jim wanted to talk some more about where they might be located, but at that moment the wheels started to turn and passengers and friends started to shout their last farewells. The Texan waved his hat once and withdrew into the carriage. He settled back in his seat, having re-collected that both Laramie and Cheyenne were further south than Jackson County, the area to which Red and Bart were heading when he parted company with them.

* * *

The journey was a long and inevitably monotonous one.

Jim passed the time by sleeping, or watching the scenery go by from the observation platform. From time to time, he indulged in a little gossip with fellow travellers. Through watching them, he observed a tension of sorts building up in them. Their hints and observations led him to believe that there was a lot of bad blood between the big ranchers and the smaller men in the counties to the east side of Wyoming.

Some of the other passengers' tension communicated itself to Jim, and he found himself scanning the platform anxiously when the train pulled into Laramie. There was no one there to meet him, and the conductor was very short with him when he finally scrambled back on board and took his seat again with an ill grace.

Thirty hours had gone by when the train reached Cheyenne, and there Jim prepared to get off the train, even if no one showed up to collect him. He made his way to the horse-box and ran out the dun which was extremely glad to be on solid ground again.

In the passengers' waiting room, a match rasped and flamed and drew his attention. It was six in the evening, and the light was good. The face which owned the thin hard lips holding the smoke seemed familiar to him. He looked again, and recognised it from another time. The man was pale and hard-eyed. Smallpox had disfigured him at an early age.

He was Slim Meldrum, a tall gunman, who had at one time enhanced his reputation in and around Amarillo, in northern Texas. Decked out in a complete black outfit with two thonged-down guns, Meldrum looked exactly what he was, a thoroughly cold-blooded and ruthless killer.

Jim followed Meldrum's eyes. He saw another man of a similar type, who was also in his middle thirties. This one, Dixie Bracknell, was almost as tall as

Meldrum. He was easy to remember because he had a seemingly flattened face. His long nose had suffered most in the flattening process. He snorted through it when he exerted himself.

Between the two was a short, stocky individual behind a fresh copy of the local newspaper. The conductor appeared at Jim's elbow. His aged face showed that he was relieved to have arrived at Cheyenne.

'There's a fellow over towards the barrier lookin' for you, young fellow. Seems your troubles are over. I'll say so long an' leave you to sort things out.'

Jim shook the gnarled hand and made for the barrier. There, he found a portly, grey-moustached man in his early fifties. His contact had on an expensive black felt hat and a grey buttoned vest. Being only a few inches over five feet in height, he had the habit of throwing back his head in an effort to look taller.

'Howdy, stranger, I figure you must be Jim Storme. Heard a few things about you over the telegraph from Vic Conners over in Idaho. I've got a feelin' you're jest the type of young fellow we need at this time in our history. Come on, let's get you out of the station an' along to your hotel!'

Jim reacted pleasantly enough. He walked along holding the dun by the head and attempted to weigh up the man who had met him. Just as the newcomer was about to speak, his guide said: 'By the way, I ought to have said sooner. My name is Milt Dodge. I'm secretary to the Wyomin' Cattlemen's Association. We're quite a powerful body, as you'll come to know. You'll be workin' for us, of course.'

Jim nodded deferentially. 'Mister Dodge, I think I ought to make it clear, I don't know much about the job, or what it is you want done. I'd like to know more about it before I say definitely that I want to work for you an' your association.'

Dodge came to a halt. He stuck his thumbs into his vest and gave Jim a long appraising look. 'Son, you're a cautious man, an' that's good. But you don't have anythin' to bother about. Everythin' will be explained tomorrow. Tonight all you have to do is rest up. As a matter of fact, we're employin' quite a few of you Texans, so you'll feel quite at home, even though you're in Wyomin'. All you need to know is how to ride well, an' how to use a gun when the occasion arises, an' I *know* you can do those two things!'

Dodge beamed at him, and Jim decided to go along with the offer, at least as far as the night's lodging at the hotel. Just as they were about to move forward again, three men pushed past him. Two of them were the hard-eyed men he had spotted in the waiting room, and the third, he presumed, was the man who had been standing behind the newspaper.

Meldrum and Bracknell gave him long glances of frank appraisal. Surprisingly, Dodge nodded to them, as though they were important to him. To the third man, who had the black coat, white shirt and string tie favoured by gamblers, Dodge called out:

'Well, howdy, Doc, you've been takin' a little exercise, I see?'

The man who answered to Doc turned and grinned at Dodge. He patted the maroon vest which was buttoned low inside his coat. 'Sure, sure, Mister Dodge, jest a short walk to watch the comings an' goings. This town sure is an interestin' place to be put down in.'

The distance between them widened. Almost as an afterthought, the man in the gambler's garb called: 'Got to make the best of our time, you know. See you tomorrow, as arranged!'

Dodge nodded and grinned and returned his attention to Jim. 'As I was sayin', son, you'll be in interestin' company when you rub shoulders with the others. Believe me, I should know.'

Jim was troubled as he settled in at the hotel. He was thinking over all the hints the travellers had given him on his rail journey. Hints about bad blood between the big ranchers and the small men and bad rustlers. He knew for sure that his brother Red was not the man to throw in with the big spread owners.

He wondered if any of this Wyoming range trouble would affect his future.

3

Jim slept well and ate good food at the Two Star Hotel, where the proprietor treated him as though he were a valuable client. An hour later than he usually finished breakfast, the Texan was enjoying a small cigar in the dining room when his contact of the previous day, Milton Dodge, came to call for him.

Dodge eyed him over quickly and thoroughly, and enquired how he had slept. Jim replied appreciatively, and asked when would be the time to talk business. Dodge mopped his grey moustache with a kerchief and beamed.

'Like I said yesterday, today you'll be put in possession of all the facts. Jest as soon as you say we'll mosey over to the Cheyenne Central Hotel where one or two important people are waitin' to make your acquaintance.'

Jim nodded and rose to his feet. He was wondering where else in the United States a cowhand would be welcomed from his breakfast in a hotel to meet very important gents in another hotel, who badly wanted him to work for them.

An attendant met Dodge in the foyer of the larger hotel and received a tip for his attempt at being helpful. The older man slowed on the way up the stairs, as his breathing was affected.

Out of the side of his mouth, he murmured: 'You see the way the ordinary folks treat us here, Jim? Believe me, you're movin' in an important part of society from now on! Jest follow me, an' be polite.'

Jim slowed his pace to keep behind, adjusted his hat and looked around him as Dodge came to a halt at one of the rooms at the front of the hotel. The sound of voices came through the ornate panelled door as the Association secretary hesitated. He straightened his necktie, gave Jim a cautionary glance, and knocked. No one answered, but he turned the knob, opened the door and ushered Jim before him.

Towards the far end of a room which was rather over-furnished, two men in their fifties were sprawled out in comfortable chairs smoking cigars.

Dodge cleared his throat. 'Howdy, gents, I see the Captain ain't arrived yet, so if you're busy I'll take this here young fellow out for a little more fresh air.'

The younger of the two, who had thinning brown hair parted high and brushed forward, started to chuckle. He reclipped his pince-nez spectacles and brushed his moustache. The older man was more heavily featured. His crown was bald, but he made up for the lack of hair by wearing a full greying moustache and beard. These men were, respectively, Richard Wall, rancher and livestock commissioner, and Senator Bob Cleave, who also had a ranch in the local county.

Cleave waved his cigar and suggested that Wall and he should have a look at the new recruit until the Captain arrived. Dodge acquiesced. Half-way across the room, Jim became aware that the wall at the back had glass across it from waist height upwards. In the room beyond were the three men he had seen on the station platform, along with perhaps two dozen other tough-looking hired hands.

'Come and sit down, young fellow,' Commissioner Wall suggested, 'you can make the acquaintance of the other men later.'

Dodge pushed a chair towards Jim, who sat down rather gingerly on the edge of it and tried to think how he was to answer these glib-tongued men with their political outlook. Dodge began to feed them details about Jim, which he had obviously learned from Conners over the telegraph. He took no pleasure in hearing a garbled version of his night clash with Lon West, but the listeners were impressed.

Dodge faltered to a stop as Jim held up his hand.

'Gents, it's mighty nice to meet you, but I'm a plain speakin' man, an' this far I haven't said much. Will you tell me this? Is the hirin' of me, an' other men like me on account of our gun prowess, or because we know a lot about cow handlin'?'

Commissioner Wall raised his brows, but he turned his head and deferred to the senator who massaged his rubbery face before answering.

'Mister Storme, I'd say the handlin' of guns was equally as important as a knowledge of cows. How does that suit you for a straight answer? We think you're the kind of man we want, otherwise you wouldn't be sharin' this room with us. The fact is, Dick Wall, here, an' me, an' a good many other ranchers in this state are sadly troubled by rustlers. An' right now is the time when we are goin' to do somethin' about it. The men we hire at five dollars a day, an' expenses, will have to use their guns before they punch cows.

'But then the men they use guns on

are rustlers, men black-listed by the livestock association, so honest cow-punchers don't need to have any conscience on that score.'

The senator paused for breath and also to see how Jim was taking this kind of talk.

Jim shrugged. Obviously he did not like the trend of the talk. He gestured with his hands. 'Senator, in a big state like the one I come from a good many of the big ranchers always seem to think that the small ones were rustlers before they made any headway. I'd like to think that your association don't think that way in Wyomin'.

'An' when it comes to shootin' down these men on the black list, I wonder how you will avoid trouble? I appreciate that the commissioner, here, an' your-self are important people, but when you start shootin' on any scale at all, there's bound to be an outcry. Any cry from the people is bound to be heard by the governor, an' he can call in the military to protect the small ranchers and such.

How will that affect you?'

Both notables showed by their expressions that they were keen to answer this pertinent query.

Dick Wall tapped the arm of his chair. 'We were careful in compilin' our list, Jim. An' recent legislation gives livestock commissioners the power to go against suspected rustlers an' appropriate their stock to offset the expense of the operation. That's what we are about to do. As for the governor, Cy Beaumont is the actin' governor of the state now, while Governor George Thompson is on sick leave.

'Beaumont sees things our way, an' so does the officer in charge of Fort Lerwick, the only military post in the district. So that about takes care of everythin'. Did you have any other query you wanted answered?'

Jim was about to point out that he had come to look for his kin, and that Red was definitely for the small men, but at that instant the door opened again, and in walked the expected leader of the coming expedition.

Captain John Verleigh was over sixty, but well preserved. He had acquired his rank and status originally in the army of the Confederate states. He was tall. His dun hat was curled at the brim sides, and his fringed buckskin outfit would have done justice to William Cody himself.

Verleigh carried a slight paunch with ease. His boring grey eyes, short grey-flecked beard and black beetle brows marked him as a born leader. He brushed through the ponderous intro-duction, and wrung Jim's hand as though the business was all settled.

Addressing himself to Jim exclusively, the Captain said: 'Son, you won't ever be expected to fire on your own kin, should such a situation arise, an' you can pull out when you wish, providin' your reason meets with my approval. Now, come along with me an' meet some of the other boys.'

Under the influence of Verleigh's strong personality, Jim went through into the next room. When the Captain introduced him, he noticed that the response of Meldrum, Bracknell and Doc Prescott was cool, if not hostile, but about half a dozen of the other hired hands crowded him close and acted as though they were affable enough.

He took a glass of whisky, answered a few straight questions and suddenly found himself one of the crowd. Two or three of their number were old enough to have served in the war between the North and South, but the majority were men born a few years later than the war; men who wanted a chance to use their weapons, and to show their superiority as marksmen over the rustlers of Jackson County and similar areas of settlement on the common land.

★   ★   ★

Two days later, the expedition set off for the north by rail.

Verleigh and the other officials in charge were deliberately vague as to their destination. Jim Storme was more unsettled than many of the hired men, as he had no idea when his brother's and his cousin's paths might not cross with the trainload of imported trouble-shooters.

The journey lasted from nine in the morning until nine in the evening, with two stops for food on the way. As the light of day was beginning to fade, they alighted at a place called Casper on the North Platte river, and there they were given their first taste of military discipline.

Captain Verleigh lined them up on the platform with their mounts and spare mounts, and looked them over, entreating them to ensure that their weapons were in the best possible order before they moved off. Two men grumbled that they were leaving town so soon after arrival, but the leader pointed out that secrecy was to play a big part in their strike against the rustlers.

After taking coffee at the depot waiting room, the men mounted up and jogged clear of town into the gathering gloom. Verleigh, it appeared, had cat's eyes. He led them down a dry stream bed, and did not let up at all until they were encamped in a remote fold in the hills, well away from the eyes of the curious.

Jim, who had asked permission to enquire about his kin in town, and been refused, slept badly. The more he thought about this expedition, approved, as it apparently was, by men in high places, the more he disliked it.

He was forthright enough to mention something of his feelings to men hunkered around his fire after Verleigh had retired for the night. One or two of the riders appeared to be mildly in sympathy with his views, but the atmosphere changed when Doc Prescott recounted the gist of what had been said to Meldrum and Bracknell.

The two deadly gunmen came and crowded Jim close by the fire. They nudged him, almost daring him to pull a weapon and shoot it out with them. He withstood the temptation, knowing that he stood no chance against the three of them, and that if anything happened to him his body could be easily disposed of in the unusual circumstances of the expedition.

He kept his temper and his patience with an effort, and soon the two Texans tired of goading him. They backed off and shared the contents of a flask with the third member of their trio. As the other men quietened, so the voices of the trio seemed to grow louder.

Meldrum was doing the talking. He murmured: 'Hey, Doc, you recall how the Captain was sayin' we'd merit a fifty dollar bonus if we personally shot one of the rustlers on the black list?'

'Sure, I recollect that, Slim,' the gambler-gunman drawled. 'Why do you ask?'

'Oh, I was thinkin' Mister Dodge might pay out the same amount if we shot one of our own number, in the event he turned out to be chicken, that's all!'

Obviously, the talk was aimed at Jim, tightly rolled in his blanket. Dixie Bracknell was slow to get the message, but when he did, he laughed a seemingly uncontrollable high-pitched laugh. There was more than a touch of hysteria in his make-up which made Jim shudder.

As sleep eluded him for a time, Jim reflected on what he had been able to pick up about the most prominent trio among the gun fighters. Meldrum was, as he had known previously, a killer of great notoriety originally from the Amarillo area of Texas. Bracknell was known and wanted in several places. Doc Prescott, the oldest of the three, had never doctored men, nor had he explored the insides of their mouths. Early on in his nefarious career, he had doctored a few cows, in the absence of a real veterinary, and that was where his title had come from. He had killed fellow gamblers rather monotonously around Wichita Falls at one time, and it was there that his reputation had been born.

Eventually, Jim fell asleep wondering what had brought the trio together.

* * *

If the hired guns were kept in the dark, others were alert on the expedition's business as Captain Verleigh wanted an early strike against the enemy before the whereabouts of his outfit became known. While the majority of the hired men lazed about, sleeping or fishing, the Captain conferred constantly in his tent with Milton Dodge, and waited for a message which did not come. Almost a day dragged by.

Dodge, who tended to live on his nerves in time of stress, at last remonstrated with the tall leader. 'Verleigh, it ain't any real good carryin' on the way you do over this business with the sheriff an' his officers. After all, it's the rustlers we're after, not the badge toters. We're secure from them with the backin' we have!'

Verleigh interrupted his pacing and turning a gimlet eye in Dodge's direction. 'You fool, Dodge! Talkin' that way shows you don't have any grasp of how this expedition has to function! Don't you realise that if the peace officers are knocked out there'll be no one to rally the settlers? Don't you think that is important, nay vital to our success?'

Dodge appeared to shrink into his chair. He began to see what was bothering his partner. The sheriff of the immediate county was a formidable man with the interests of the small ranchers and settlers at heart. If he got wind of what was afoot, he could do a lot to stir up the settlers against the small army of the association.

The tent was quiet when one of the armed team coughed by the door and murmured that a rider was on his way in. Verleigh at once took a grip of himself. He asked Dodge with grave politeness to stand by the door, while he himself sat behind the table which held the local maps and endeavoured to appear calm.

The scout, or spy, who came in rather breathlessly, was anything but a prepossessing figure. Jerry Jones was nearly fifty. He looked older, being a weathered man in shabby trail clothes with a straggly beard. He had a way of crouching as he stood in the tent, and his body appeared to be shrunken under a large black hat with a broken brim.

Verleigh was disappointed. He revealed as much in a long sigh.

'All right, Jerry, I suppose you'd better tell me what you've learned, but I won't deny I'd be better pleased if you were bringin' news from the county seat.'

Jones squatted on the edge of a wooden seat, and shot a sharp glance at Dodge. 'No word from the six men who went against the peace officers?' he enquired huskily.

Verleigh shook his head, and Jones delivered himself of his information. 'I don't rightly think that small ranch, the Lazy K, is the place to make your first strike, Captain. Fact is, there's a whole lot of unnecessary activity in an' around the spot. Almost as though they'd had a tip-off about your special interest in their boss.'

'What is this special activity?' Verleigh queried.

'They're puttin' up earthworks like the civil war was on again, an' throwin' up a ring of stakes, too. Almost as though they'd been forewarned, like I was sayin'. On the other hand, I could tell you a good alternative where you couldn't fail to make an impression, if you're interested!'

Jones waited, chewing his lip, while Verleigh referred to his map and his notes.

'You mean Vance's place, don't you?'

'Sure, that's the name. Vance is a bachelor. He works hard an' he only has one man with him. A tall fellow by the name of Big Sandy. They work most of the time an' don't often move into town. You could take 'em at your fancy. If they've been warned, they ain't takin' any notice. No sir, no notice at all.'

Verleigh was nodding steadily. Already he was seeing the small Vance place as the focal point of his first strike. Jones cut through his thoughts with a disquieting query.

'I suppose nobody from here could have tipped off the men at the Lazy K, Captain?'

Verleigh frowned and glanced across at Dodge. 'I don't think it could be so. Apart from the party that went off to tackle the peace officers, only one man has been away from camp. Storme, the fellow from Idaho. An' he rode towards the east, which would keep him well away from the Lazy K, an' Vance's place.'

Jones seemed satisfied with this explanation. So did Dodge, and presently a change came over Verleigh as he began to think out in detail how he would strike the Vance place, and eliminate the men located there.

Jim Storme came into camp a half-hour later.

Before he was allowed to relax, he was ordered to give a full account of his meanderings during the day, and all he had seen. As far as scouting was concerned, Jim had learned little. The country to the east was relatively calm, and thinly populated. Verleigh's last question surprised him.

'No, sir, I didn't see or hear of anythin' to do with my kin.'

Dismissed from the tent, Jim found Meldrum and his sidekicks quite interested in his little sojourn away from the camp, but he told them almost nothing of what had transpired within the tent. Just when the trio were beginning to get a little nasty, Dodge stuck his head out of the canvas erection and called for Doc Prescott. Meldrum and Bracknell rose to their feet and went with him.

They were obviously pleased to be called into the presence of the leader.

4

Sweetwater City, the county seat of Jackson County, Wyoming, was some fifteen miles away from the spot where the association's invaders were hunkered down and spoiling for trouble.

Sweetwater sported a town marshal's office in addition to that of the county sheriff, but there was no doubt in the minds of the townsfolk which of the local peace officers was the top man. The town marshal was known to have friends among certain large scale ranchers in the district, while Sheriff Amos Grant, who neither sought nor asked for special favours anywhere, was branded as the friend of the underdog by those who disliked his special brand of justice.

Grant was a dark-haired stooping man, thin-featured and with a tuft of chin beard to render him more striking.

He wore a floppy black stetson and a vest of the same colour, hiding a white shirt and a string tie. An injury suffered early in his adult life left him with a slight limp which was immediately apparent to everyone because he was so restless.

The day after Jim Storme did his scouting trip, Sheriff Grant was in his office, along with Bart McGivern, who had recently become his chief deputy. Bart kept turning to pace every new direction in the office as Grant paced. In so doing, he dwarfed his senior officer with his height advantage of three inches and the overwhelming size of his shoulders.

★　★　★

Bart remarked: 'The townsfolk will be bangin' on the door again any minute, Amos. Have you thought what you are goin' to say to them?'

Grant stopped in his pacing. He was annoyed. 'I don't have to make up my mind what to say, Bart, an' you know it.

I've never compromised before, an' I don't aim to start now, so help me.'

Bart crossed the floor on his long legs and took a look through the barred grille in the door of the cells' passage. The two unkempt ruffians in the first cell were standing up, rather defiantly, and obviously wondering how good were their chances of being freed, if the townsfolk kept up their badgering of the sheriff.

Bart gave them a sour grin and backed away again.

Grant remarked. 'Old Sam Widdens is too good-natured. Findin' them two ornery cusses prowlin' his stables made Sam mad for the first time in his life. Of course they intended to lift his hosses! If they hadn't been slightly liquored to start with he'd never have caught them. An' now we have 'em behind bars, an' because there's all this talk about the Stockgrowers' Association bringin' in hired guns to shoot up the small men an' clear the range again for the big ones, Sam's done a lot of listenin' an' they've turned him soft! I won't listen to them!'

The hammering on the front door commenced again at that moment.

Grant grunted. He picked up his rifle and stalked over to the door, pulling out the holding bar and stepping on to the sidewalk boards with Bart at his back. He sighed, and yawned shortly afterwards. Upwards of twenty men, in a thick crescent all around Sam Widdens, waited as though requesting permission to state their case.

'Jest listen to Sam, will you, Sheriff?' a voice pleaded from the back, 'an listen good!'

'I know what Sam Widdens wants, but I'll listen to him jest the same, if it'll make you all feel good!'

Widdens, in his middle fifties, red-faced and white-haired, began to grow breathless when he thought about saying his piece. Grant had to wait for him a little longer.

'Sheriff, I want you to release those two men I brought in yesterday. I'm bound to say I think I acted a little hastily. Like they pleaded, they may be down on their luck, an' they didn't actually steal anythin', did they?'

'Sam, these two prisoners of mine have got rustler written all over them. Nothin' will ever convince me that they ended up in your stables to do you a favour. The only reason they didn't steal anythin' was because you blundered in on them before they were ready to do their work! An' another thing. The law ain't a thing to be switched on an' off jest when a man thinks about it, either.

'I'm keepin' those jaspers in that cell until they can be arraigned in court, an' what's more, Sam, you're goin' to tell your story the way you told it when you came into town. I'm not goin' soft, even if *you* are!'

'Nobody wants you to go soft, Sheriff, only in these days when the big ranchers call all us smaller men rustlers so they can blast us offen the range, surely this is a time to close our ranks.

Even rustlers might come in handy, if we have to fight for our lives an' our property!'

Grant cleared his throat when the chorus of approval had died down. 'That last one is an interestin' theory, but it don't influence me. How do you know I wouldn't take an unfair advantage of you to ingratiate myself with the big boys, if I allowed rustlers to go free for reasons of sentiment?'

'Aw heck, Amos,' Widdens protested. 'We know you better than that!'

'You ought to have been a politician, Sheriff, not a gun toter!'

This latter unidentified voice raised the ghost of a smile on the sheriff's face. Bart noticed it and looked away, in case his own expression turned a situation of gravity into one of levity.

Grant said his piece once again, quite forcefully. He concluded by asking permission, in a sarcastic tone of voice, to re-enter his office without interruption, so that he could resume his efforts to ramrod the county without interference.

The crowd, including Sam Widdens, backed off with a marked show of reluctance. Sam bought a free round of drinks in the nearest saloon, but even that could not take out of men's thoughts their basic dread of an imported army of guns to be lined up against them and theirs.

* * *

Food was brought in for the disappointed prisoners.

Sheriff and deputy stretched their legs in turn, and then settled back in their place of work to eat their supper together.

'Tell me, Amos, do you think there's any substance in the latest crop of rumours? Would the association actually try to eliminate the likes of you an' me?'

Grant masticated his food slowly. When his mouth was empty, he nodded. 'I'd say the association would, because with the likes of you an' me out of the way there'd be nobody to rally the settlers against the invaders.'

He fingered his chin beard, before continuing.

'If you really want to know my thoughts, Bart, I'd say somethin' serious was meant to happen to you an' me last night.'

Bart gasped and dropped his fork on the floor. He retrieved it slowly and thoughtfully, as he relived the events of the previous day. Late in the afternoon, they had received an urgent summons to an isolated homestead belonging to a man named Drummond, an Englishman. The message had said that gunshots had come from the shack, and that Drummond was believed to be dead.

Thinking that the invasion might have begun, sheriff and deputy had set off together, leaving their jailer in charge of the office. Quite by chance, they had encountered the man, Drummond, on the way to his homestead. He had started out a day earlier to drive up country in his wagon to visit his sister, but a jug of moonshine had been his temporary downfall, and his wife and children had begun to think they would never cover the ten miles.

'Drummond really did have a broken wheel on his cart when we overtook him, Amos. The rest of the story might have been true.'

Grant nodded soberly. 'On the other hand, it might have been a complete fabrication. I sent Milner's boy over to Drummond's place this morning, an' he said there was signs of several riders havin' visited the place an' their havin' hunkered down as though they were waitin' for somebody.'

'You think it was an ambush party, waitin' for you an' me?'

'I most certainly do, but I'd like to have you keep it to yourself, Bart. Trouble will make itself known, all too soon.'

In spite of himself, Big Bart shuddered. His appetite waned at that moment and he started to think about

Red Storme and how he was fixed. A knock of a different kind ended a brooding silence some fifteen minutes later. In answer to the sheriff's call, a gaunt old man who had prospected in the county for nearly thirty years stepped inside.

'Sheriff, will you be tellin' me if Drummond the Englishman is over to his home?'

'So far as I know, Monty, he's away up country with his family to stay with his sister for a few days. They're havin' a weddin' or somesuch.'

'I'm glad,' the old man replied abruptly. 'I'm thinkin' Drummond's had bad luck in his absence. I've been smellin' wood burnin' since shortly after midday, an' it all blows across from Drummond's direction. Sorry to bear bad news. If I'd been younger I'd have been over there to see what I could do about the blaze. As it is, there can't be much left.'

Bart wanted to ask Monty a whole lot of questions, but Amos made a negative gesture, and the restless old man left shortly afterwards with Grant's thanks ringing in his ears.

'You don't think the fire was an accident,' Bart remarked accusingly, when they were alone again.

'Do you?' the sheriff retorted, sticking his bunched fists on his hips.

Bart signified his agreement.

They were slow to get to their bunks that night. Neither of them expected to sleep. In the hour before midnight, they had two reports from cowed wayfarers who had been slow to pass on what they had learned. One report told of a farmer and his family killed by gunshot wounds in their house on the banks of the North Platte. The second told of newcomers, two brothers who had been in the act of erecting their home on the opposite bank of the same river when the killers struck.

The invasion forces had struck. Where would they strike next?

5

As had been anticipated by both sides, news of the first offensive strike spread like wildfire. Tension built up in the score of men who still lingered in the hollow where they had been since leaving the train. Although their hiding place was well chosen, they had the naked sort of feeling commonly felt by men whose business is not strictly legal.

Captain Verleigh sent Milton Dodge into the midst of the restless gunmen to talk to them during the midday meal. The association secretary took his task quite seriously, spending far more time talking than eating in an attempt to calm the trigger-tempered gunmen who were suffering because they had not had a chance to try their weapons.

'Where are the first six men who rode out from here?' Doc Prescott asked bluntly.

Dodge was slow to answer. 'That we don't know, as yet. But they must have been in action because we know for certain that many rustlers have been killed, an' that one small ranch, at least, has been burned down!'

'I can't see why they haven't been back here to make a claim for the extra money connected with deaths,' Meldrum added, as he savaged a beef sausage. 'They were in this for money jest the same as the rest of us.'

He glanced round to gather support to his line of argument, but in doing so, his eyes encountered a glance from Dodge, and something in the older man's glance made him think again about furthering his argument. He awaited Dodge's reply.

'When men go away from the main party on an expedition such as they were on, they have to use their initiative. We have to remember that we are the invaders. Although we are makin' the prime moves there will be times when it is necessary to take evasive action. In any case, members of the association like to think that their hired men are interested in what they are tryin' to do, an' not jest in collectin' big money for a little sharpshootin'.'

The duty cooks brought forward another big tray full of cooked food, which fed men's bodies and kept their tongues busy with the exercise of mastication.

Jim was one of the first to eat his fill. He waved his fork in Dodge's direction, and called across the cooking fire to him.

'Mister Dodge, can you tell us for certain whether the Captain has any sort of a plan for the rest of us actually in mind at this moment?'

At the risk of stealing Verleigh's thunder, Dodge nodded and smiled. 'The Captain had a plan fully detailed long before the sun was up today. But he'll want to tell you about it himself. So I won't anticipate what he's goin' to say. Believe me, this period of inactivity is almost over, an' you'll have all the work you want, an' more!'

Dodge slipped away about ten minutes later. Towards three in the afternoon, a messenger risked antagonising the resting groups by shaking every man and announcing that the Captain would be along to address all men in ten minutes.

★ ★ ★

Verleigh had obviously spruced himself up for the occasion.

His beard was trimmed, and his hat and clothing had been brushed. He walked the fringe of the assembled group until he found a suitable rounded hummock on which to trust his feet. He would have had their full attention if he had only been three feet tall, let alone six feet.

'Men, you will be in action before the sun sets again. The county is in uproar. Rustlers an' small settlers are pesterin' the county peace office to do somethin' about us, but this far only our friends know exactly where we are.'

Prescott hoisted his hand, showing nerve in interrupting the Captain which few of his fellows could match.

'Captain, wouldn't it be advisable for us to do somethin' about the sheriff an' his immediate staff?'

Verleigh's eyes found and sought those of Dodge, before he answered.

'Boys, we have a strategist in our midst. The fact is, Doc, the first six men away from here were supposed to eliminate the sheriff. Somethin' must have gone wrong with that plan. But we can't write off our fellows as a dead loss. Things have been happenin' towards the east which could only have been carried out by our group. And, incidentally, they've drawn the investigatin' peace officers in that direction an' kept them away from this hideout!

'The plan I have in mind for you is a strike against a small ranch, where there are only two men. I aim to use all of you, to give you a little practice with your firearms, but I don't anticipate much trouble in oustin' the two settlers, an' firin' their property.'

At this stage, Verleigh paused and made a throwaway gesture in the direction of a cart which had appeared the previous evening. He did not explain the significance of the vehicle at that time. Nor did anyone ask for an explanation. They were all intensely keen to hear about their strike. The leader went on to explain the exact location of the small ranch which was situated close to slow moving water within five miles.

'What are the names of the two men involved?' Jim called out, during a pause for breath.

'Well,' Verleigh went on, 'one of them is called Vance, Paul Vance, I think. He's a ruddy-faced fellow in his late thirties with a lot of fair curly hair.'

He hesitated before mentioning the other man, and Dodge, clearing his throat very consciously, butted in. 'The name of the other man is a little obscure. He's been in these parts for quite some time, an' the locals call him Big Sandy. That satisfy you, Storme?'

Jim wanted to ask for a full description of Big Sandy, but Verleigh used his strong personality to make him give a grudging nod. Jim's interest waned. It picked up again a few minutes later, when the leader was back discussing the details of the raid.

'Understand this. When the time comes to strike I want you all to fire off a few rounds. But if the two men get wind of our approach we'll have to do it differently. I reckon the best way to tackle the job would be to have four hands, detailed off beforehand, to undertake the actual stormin' of the place an' the elimination of the settlers.'

He had to stop because of the sudden outbreak of talk in groups over the chance to acquire the fifty dollar bonuses for the men on the association list. After waiting for two minutes, he cleared his throat and talked them down.

'All right, men, that's enough. On

second thoughts, I don't think I'll detail anybody. I'll leave it to your good sense to pick out four men to do the rough work if the opposition gets warnin'.'

With that, he adjusted his hat, stepped down off his hummock and backtracked towards his tent to put the finishing touches to the plan for the elimination of Vance, his partner and his ranch.

*   *   *

Even before the Captain was back in his tent, and before Dodge could get clear of the hired hands, they were arguing and pointing at each other like excited schoolboys; except that their hands were constantly going down towards their gun belts while their eyes hardened.

Meldrum, Bracknell and Prescott were as keen as anyone, but they were thinking more than the others. They backed to one side of the heaving group, shoulder to shoulder, and faced the rest of the outfit in that way with their hands all low and at the ready. Prescott, the shortest of the trio, was in the middle.

Meldrum yelled for quietness. The others grudgingly gave it. Meldrum's pale face held their attention for upwards of a minute, and then his hard eyes slid away to Bracknell. The latter grinned, then frowned and grinned again. He giggled, and in his inimitable high-pitched voice, made an announcement.

'Gents, one an' all, we think it's about time we let you know that we've come to a decision. The Doc is about to do the explainin'.'

Doc Prescott showed no signs of emotion whatever. He went on in a very matter of fact voice. 'Fellow riders, my pardners an' me, we have decided to spearhead this attack the Captain told us about. If you feel you have anythin' to discuss with us, now is the time to say so.'

He might have been chairman of a council meeting, but the tension was there just the same. Jim moved a little to one side, and tried to see the assembled men from the viewpoint of those who had just issued the challenge. The first minute or two were critical. Then, it gradually became clear, no one was goin' to challenge them. Eventually, a hard-riding loner from Arizona slowly raised his hand and broke the silence.

'If you gents are headin' this strike force, you are only three, an' four are wanted. How about the fourth man?'

This time it was Meldrum who chuckled. 'Don't build up your hopes unduly, mister. My buddies an' me, we tend to have favourites. We'll tell you who the fourth man is later. Right now, we're goin' to confer with the Captain.'

They did a good job in withdrawing and heading for the tent without stumbling, and at the same time kept their attention upon the men they had just left. The trio were admitted to the tent with the minimum of delay.

*　*　*

Jim was disturbed by the latest development. He realised that Meldrum and his sidekicks were making a definite bid to lead the hired gunmen under Verleigh's authority. He also knew that their attitude towards himself was as deadly as it could possibly be. The talk of a Big Sandy was baffling. Red Storme was big and sandy-haired, but then Wyoming was a big state. Even the county of Jackson was widespread. And Red and Bart had not attempted to write to him since they put their roots down. Either or both of them might have decided that Wyoming was not for them. They could have moved on well over a year ago, and never come back to this region. This line of reasoning, however, did not minimise Jim's anxiety. A man was lucky if he had kin these days, and Red represented his only close kin. Bearing this in mind, he — Jim — ought to act as though Big Sandy *was* Red, and do his utmost to counter any plan to kill him.

He thought about waiting until the Meldrum trio had left the tent and then going over to Verleigh to ask for his freedom. But somehow, in spite of what the Captain had said when they first met, he could not see the leader allowing him to simply pack his gear and ride away at such a vital stage in the invasion.

Verleigh had covered himself by saying that a man's reason to go would have to meet with his approval. Any man riding away from the hired army at this time was a potential source of danger to it. Especially a man who was intent on finding his kin among the recent settlers.

No, Verleigh would not let him go. And where did that leave him?

One other way of being helpful to the two men lined up for attack was to go along with Meldrum and the other two and spearhead the attack on the ranch. He figured that his chances of being picked as the fourth man in the small strike force were nil.

After that, his attempt at planning floundered. The only other way in which he could help the beleaguered was to get well to the back, sound the alarm and try and foul up the efforts of the men in advance of him by simulated inaccurate shooting. And that meant the same thing as shooting men in the back, a most distasteful consideration.

Hunkered as he was, at the foot of a tree, Jim groaned without knowing it. He rolled himself a fat smoke, and puffed at it steadily. When he had smoked it to the butt, he rubbed it out on his boot heel and gradually sank into a fitful doze.

In fact, he actually slept for a short while.

He awoke to see a black pointed boot toe quite close to his thigh and head. He had seen the expensive footwear before. It belonged to Meldrum, whose leg was in it at that time. Flanking Meldrum were the obvious pair, and behind the trio stood about ten other men, stiff with excitement.

Slim's eyes were like polished bullet tips as he stared down at Jim. 'Storme,' he began, 'we wanted you to be the first to hear the glad news. We've decided to take you along as the fourth member of the strike team. How does the idea suit you? We'll be pullin' out along with the others in half an hour.'

Jim cleared his dry throat. His pulse was racing and so were his thoughts, but he contrived to keep the intense excitement out of his face as he answered.

'I suppose I ought to thank you for puttin' the opportunity my way when so many others wanted it. So thanks. But right now I'm takin' a nap, so if you'll back off with that fancy foot gear of yours, I'll be obliged.'

He closed his eyes again, and worked to keep his eyelids from fluttering. Somehow he succeeded long enough. Meldrum hesitated for a long time, toying with the idea of annoying the lone Texan, but something made him turn up this marvellous opportunity. Perhaps it was some thought about the future. Meldrum backed off and walked with his minions to the place where their horses were pegged out. One or two of the others went after them, and Jim was left alone.

When he was sure he had ceased to be the main attraction, he opened his eyes and peered around him. In asking for him to go along with them, the top guns had solved some of his problems. He would be up in front, after all; but this move on the part of the trio did not fool him. He did not know what they had in mind for him. All he knew was that a head-on clash would come sooner or later, and if it came sooner he could perhaps help society at large by eliminating one or more of them before they got him.

Such an act would be some consolation if he failed to locate and aid brother Red.

6

A little over ninety minutes after Jim had been given his startling news the stock growers' army was in position to strike. Within a furlong of the creek known as Little Platte, the big cart acquired by the invaders was backed into a copse, along with its four shaft horses.

Sixteen men had been sent away on foot to put a distant half-circle round the small ranch which backed its home area on to the near side of the creek. The water itself was fairly broad and swift-running, making the surrounding of the establishment in broad daylight a difficult thing to accomplish.

Scrub pine and oaks, dotted here and there on the slope down to the water, partially obscured the view of the four crude buildings which made up the ranch.

Jim and the Meldrum trio went forward in a line, ahead of the other gunmen. Jim was on the north flank, and the other three were strung out to the south of him. Within five minutes of the slow ghosting forward, Jim and Bracknell caught a brief glimpse of Vance as he came out to the pump and retired again. He was tall, hefty, and ruddy-faced as they had been told earlier, and being hatless they saw at once the luxuriance of his over-long curly fair hair.

Jim's heart leapt at the sight of him. Uppermost in his mind was a deep desire to know if this was the sort of man, or indeed *the* man, with whom his brother had thrown in his lot. Vance's abrupt return indoors prevented the precipitation of action. The rancher had seen nothing to alert him.

Jim thought about and discarded half a dozen simple plans for making the rancher aware of the danger, but each he knew would arouse Meldrum's suspicion and perhaps bring about an early disaster. So he bided his time, and fate came to his aid. Something happened in the copse where the cart was hidden. The attackers found out afterwards that a small snake had startled the shaft horses. Obviously, they were very frightened.

The tinkle of harness echoed down the slope, and the sounds of animals thrashing about and kicking one another. It was all the warning the two men wanted. Meldrum and his partners cursed quietly, while Jim strained his eyes forward, and rubbed the curve which made his nose Roman in shape.

For a mere second or so, a lean face, taut with anxiety and with the fine dark eyebrows drawn down close, appeared at a small window on the near side of the biggest building. It might, or might not have been that of Red Storme. Jim kept shaking his head, as though his troubled imagination was definitely playing tricks with him.

The hair on the observer's head had been long and straight, and seemingly light in colour. It could have been sandy, though, when the best light of day was on it. The face came and went in a flash. And then a voice cried out, demanding to know if anyone was in trouble.

No answer, of course. Then the thick door was thrown open, back from the narrow gallery. A hand and nose were withdrawn, and a voice of a different calibre shouted: 'What's goin' on back there? If you're honest, show yourself!'

There was excitement behind the voice, but no suggestion of panic. Meldrum and his buddies went into action like a well-practised orchestra. Slim himself sent his first rifle bullet through the pane of glass where the face had showed. Bracknell, by contrast, concentrated on the door, firing first at knee level and then where the enquirer's head ought to have been.

Needless to record, Vance did not leave any part of his body to absorb the fusillade. By the time Prescott was stitching the door and the front of the shack with bullet holes, the owner was already reaching across with a plank behind the door in an effort to close and secure it with the minimum of delay.

Bracknell yelled out like a drunken cowboy yahooing a trail town. He pumped shells at the gaps between the logs, and Jim, mindful of his role, put two careful bullets into the sloping roof. Almost at once, the bullets began to come back at them.

The advance party of attackers desisted after about three minutes, and the men who were wider out on the flanks put in their share of bullets, making a deal more noise and intentionally trying to make the defenders know that their position was hopeless.

* * *

In the shack, Paul Vance and Red Storme regarded one another as they reloaded.

'Well, this is what we bought when

we declined the offer to move in with the Lazy K boys, Red,' Vance remarked laconically. 'Apparently all the local boys' worst fears are goin' to be realised. Personally, I think you were a darned fool not to pull out when you had the chance. It ain't as if you had your roots down here, after all.'

Red slapped the barrel of his shoulder gun. 'Thanks for all that uncalled for criticism, brother, an' who's goin' to cook the next meal?'

Red fired off two shots through the shattered window space before he heard any sort of a reply from Vance.

'Unless I'm mistaken, all the shootin' is on our side of the creek. The noise will spook our cattle further away on the other side, make 'em hard to locate an' round-up, if that's what is behind all this action. I still can't believe the livestock association is ruthless enough to try an' wipe us out!'

As though to help change his mind, a ricochet hit a beam above Vance's head and sent the flattened bullet down towards him. It hit the extremity of his left shoulder blade, chipping the bone in the process, and making a painful groove for about three inches down the outside of his arm.

'What does it take to convince you, amigo?' Red enquired, as he slithered across the floor in an effort to help.

'All right, all right, so I withdraw what I said before the ricochet arrived. If you want to get out of this homestead in one piece, the time is about now. Don't kid yourself Sheriff Grant will be here with help before these jaspers out front eliminate us! Our luck has about run out! The ranch will have to go, regardless of the work we've put in on it!'

Red wound a clean bandanna tightly around the wound and made Paul wince. He put a stop to any sort of talk about their splitting up. Red knew that Paul would not be driven off his property unless matters grew a whole lot worse, and he had no intention of leaving his employer and friend in the lurch.

Some ten minutes later, there was

a slight lull, while the attackers reappraised the position, and took time out for a smoke. As soon as they were sure what was happening, the beleaguered men did exactly the same.

Red prowled the single storey building in an effort to find out if there was anything of which they were desperately short. All they required, it seemed, was more water, and the pump was away to one side of the building rather than behind it; which made for a special sort of problem.

'We need the big can,' Red murmured. 'I left it under the pump, gosh durn it, an' now is the time it has to come back. We may not get another breathin' space.'

Vance came up off the floor, where he had been resting. 'Red, you ain't goin' to risk settin' foot out of doors to collect that can! Hear me?'

The two men knew each other very well. Red knew there was only one way in which he could get the can. He had to temporarily incapacitate Paul. He turned slowly, and then, without warning, gave him a brief clip on the jaw which sent him down on the floor again with a jolt.

★　★　★

Meanwhile, the attack drama was going through another stage.

Meldrum, five yards to Jim's right and a similar distance behind him, was giving advice. 'Storme, me an' the boys decided before we ever got into this position that you should be the one to get the first bonus. So, I'm suggestin' to you that you go ahead of Dixie an' me, with coverin' fire, of course, an' do the necessary!'

As the full purport of Slim's words sank in, Jim looked around to see where Prescott was located. He found out almost at once that during the slow crawling advance, the agile little gunman had worked his way behind him, on the other flank. It meant that Jim could be protected by the other three, or rendered vulnerable to them, in the event they turned treacherous.

Prescott levered and their eye glances met.

Jim knew he was in a most invidious position. He could be an accidental write-off at any time, if Meldrum's boys intended to have him out of the way. On the other hand, if they started to keep a watch on him, it might relieve the pressure on the men in the shack.

He signified that he was willing to go along with Meldrum's suggestion, and left the shelter of his rock almost at once, pushing forward his Winchester and slithering after it. Within the following minute, Red slipped out of the back of the shack and hurled himself away from shelter in an effort to get to the pump unnoticed.

Dixie Bracknell blinked in surprise. 'Hey, Slim, did you see anybody ghost away from the shack jest then?'

Meldrum snorted. He submitted the terrain ahead of him to the closest of scrutinies, and finally passed the word forward to Jim to be doubly on the alert. Jim acknowledged and pumped a shell into the window of the shack as he pretended to see a shadow. Nothing would have made him forgive himself if he had hit the owner.

Red dashed back. Meldrum put a bullet into the earth between his legs, and Jim missed twice by a matter of six inches. He could not have hit a target at that distance just then, had he wanted to, because he had recognised his brother, and the shock had temporarily unnerved him. His fears were realised, and he still had no idea how he could turn the present situation to one less dangerous.

Vance, having recovered, fired back at Jim's new hiding place and was sufficiently accurate to ventilate the top of the dun stetson. It twisted on his head and then parted company, but only rolled a few feet behind him. The Texan leaned backwards and groped for it with the stock of his Winchester. The distraction gave him a short space in which to think, but no special ideas came.

Doc Prescott recommenced firing at the front of the house. His first bullet went within a foot of Jim, and reminded him unnecessarily of the invidiousness of his position. It was at that instant that Jim's mind went back to his boyhood when Red and he had relived made-up scenes from the war, with the first real weapons entrusted to them. They had had a private signal of gunshots. It was a signal which Jim had never forgotten. But would Red remember, and risk letting him through?

If the trick could be pulled off it might change everything. At least, Jim could turn his gun against those who were coming along behind him, and thus heighten the defenders' chances of survival.

Without giving himself time to weigh his chances, he rolled away towards his right, achieving the shelter of another rock before the bullets whined around him. He did this twice more, until he was only a few yards from the gate which gave access to the small paddock.

There, he decided, he would have to try his gun signal, or abandon the idea of trying it altogether. The signal was easy enough. It consisted of firing one rifle shot closely followed by two revolver shots. By the gate, a man had to be an exceptional shot to make a Colt effective against the house. He hoped that Meldrum would not query this; also that the deadly gunman would not wonder at the way he was fumbling with two types of guns.

He moved to the gate and hurriedly sighted along the Winchester muzzle with his .45 gripped in his right hand. Something made him think a shot was imminent from the house. He squeezed the trigger and sent a bullet into the woodwork over the nearest window. Directly afterwards he fired two revolver bullets into the wall. For want of something better to do, he then counted up to ten. His heart was thumping more than he had ever known it before.

Suddenly, the defenders retaliated. Two shots hit the top of the gatepost, well above him, and then their attention was deliberately turned to the other guns who were not so near. Jim hoped this was the indication which he had hoped for. Whether it was or not, this was the time to make his big move.

He reached up and unlatched the gate, allowing it to swing towards him. As it swung the trio behind him began to put down a steady barrage to give him cover. He marvelled that they had this far kept faith with him. He rolled under the gate, put his feet under him and went forward at a crouching run, firing off his Winchester every few seconds, but scarcely taking a proper aim.

Bullets from the house came close, but not too close. Those whining towards him from the rear went closer. One even singed his denims across the seat. That one perhaps made him call forth a last desperate effort which enabled him to fall through the window opening head first. The fall accidentally discharged the last shot out of the Winchester and made him drop the Colt.

His chin cracked against the floor and he became aware of two tense faces and unwinking gun muzzles. His head was still muzzy from his fall when Red sighed and blew out his lips in an impolite noise.

Relief was painfully apparent on the faces of the defenders as the older Storme pulled his revolver and fired three shots into the ceiling beams.

'This is my kid brother, all right, an' those shots mean he's dead, so let's take it from there. Heaven knows what's happened to his manners since he left home, or how he came to be spearheadin' a crew like we have out front.'

'Maybe he's an angel,' Vance murmured, fingering and dabbing his jaw, which had developed a thin line of blood.

'I'm Jim Storme, all right. How I

came to be mixed up with the stock growers' association is a long story which will keep. The point is I'm here, an' as long as I can turn my gun against the killers out there you two stand a chance of gettin' clear. So let's get down to some basic talk. Do you trust me?'

Jim's eyes went away to Paul Vance's. He felt sure that Red knew him well enough to know that he was not working a double-cross.

Vance replied: 'I thought you wanted to get down to the basic talk.'

Jim grinned with relief. They shook hands all round, while the invaders renewed battle.

7

For several minutes bullets ripped into the building from many angles. They came unnoticed, as Jim was rather breathlessly trying to explain how he had come to be with the invasion force and attacking the ranch. While he was still talking and Red was taking in his words, Paul Vance groaned a couple of times. The chipped bone in his shoulder was giving him a deal of pain.

Finally, the rancher sank his head against his knees on the floor as a wave of nausea attacked his senses. Red went over to him with a damp bandanna, and bathed his face and neck.

'Somehow or another I've got to get Paul out of this before the invaders overrun this place. Jest a short while ago I had to hit him on the jaw before I could slip out to fetch water.'

Jim bit his lip. 'I'll do anythin' you

like to help get him again. One of us will have to stay behind to hold the place, otherwise the hired guns will close in too quickly an' that will be an end to all of us. We shouldn't think of waitin' for outside help. Any sort of intervention will make the attackers step up the shootin'.

'So, things bein' the way they are, I'll be glad to hold off these hired guns while you slip Paul away an' get him across the water.'

Without waiting for an answer, Jim moved away on hands and knees, examining the building and wondering what its resources were in the matter of defence. It had four simple rooms, all on one level. As Jim came back to the front, Red banged with his knee on a rug underneath two legs of the table.

'There's a cellar down here, an' it's ventilated, too,' he murmured, 'but I don't figure Paul would let you stay behind on your own, especially seein' as how those buzzards would tear you apart for turnin' your gun on them.'

'That's something' we'll have to see about when the time comes,' Jim returned soberly. 'Maybe it won't come to that. Perhaps I'll have a chance to slip away when you an' him are across the creek. You'll try it, won't you, Red?'

The big sandy-haired man gnawed at the last joint of his right thumb. He was reluctant to expose his younger brother to extreme danger of this kind. He remarked: 'This is a time when we could have done with Bart. Cousin Bart, I mean, if you haven't forgotten him.'

'Any chance of him comin' along?'

'I don't think so. I don't believe anyone could get here in time to be of assistance. You were accurate in your earlier surmise. Bart is workin' with the county sheriff, though, an' he would have been a good man in a tight situation like this.'

'Good old Bart,' Jim remarked, with a sigh. He ducked as a splinter of wood was chipped out of a ceiling beam. 'They're comin' closer, an' the three boys to the front are absolutely deadly, Red.'

Vance's senses returned as they continued their task. 'Hey, Red, will you back off an' give me room to use my rifle?'

'Big Sandy, to you, Vance,' the older Storme retorted. But he pushed his employer's gun into his hand and covertly watched how he handled it. Vance fired it once, but the effort of holding it steady made his left shoulder ache. Without wanting to do so, he lowered the stock of his gun to the floor and shot an agonised glance at the other two which did not pass unnoticed.

Red remarked: 'The stock growers' men may get your place, but they don't have to get you, Paul. I'm aimin' to take you out jest as soon as you feel you can make it. An' don't argue, because if you do, the alternative will mean death for all three of us. Jim, here, is goin' to stay behind for a short while an' put up a few shots to hold up the advance. How are you feelin' now?'

Vance fretted and argued for perhaps two minutes. There was another short delay while he made sure that Jim wanted to involve himself as the lone defender, and then he agreed to leave and tersely outlined a plan.

Jim listened, but at the same time he edged nearer to the window which faced on to the scene of the action. In so doing, he was making it clear to Red that he would approve of any scheme. Presently, when he was levering and firing again, Red came to his elbow.

'Jim, I want you to know that we appreciate what it is that you are doin'. Don't hang on too long. I'll try an' get back to help you once I have Paul on his way. Take care of yourself, an' so long.'

Jim shook hands again. He added: 'If you ever get one of those buzzards in your sights, don't hesitate, Red.'

They parted and Jim heard a door open behind him, giving access to the rear part of the house. He would have liked to see the two escapers clear of the building, but he knew he dared not take such a liberty with people like Meldrum out at the front. Instead, he pulled the rug out from under the table with the intention of using it to kneel on.

It was then that he got his first true glimpse of the trapdoor which gave access to the cellar. There were steps under it and another rug and a lamp secreted in the bottom, some eight feet down. He wondered how it was ventilated, and his curiosity made him push the door all the way back and go down the steps to investigate. Let into the front and rear walls of the subterranean chamber were narrow shafts which carried to places beyond the house, letting in air and a tiny filtering of daylight.

His fingers busied themselves with a paper and tobacco sack. It appeared to him that Vance, or whoever had constructed the cabin and the cellar, had had the notion of using it to house someone. Usually, the extra space was only used for storage, and vents were exceptionally rare.

A renewed outbreak of firing cut short his speculation and sent him up the steps again to see how the attack was developing. He dearly wanted to go to the back and see if he could glimpse his brother and the wounded rancher, but such an act would have been foolhardy with Meldrum and his buddies so close in the front.

The bullets were coming from the outer ring of attackers, which seemed to suggest that the trio were advancing again, or planning to rush the place. No one was as far forward as the gate, but they could not be much further away. He wished, as he mused over the threatening situation, that he had stayed long enough to close the gate again.

As he had left it, wide open, a crawling man could slip through it without difficulty, provided that the supporting guns were firing at the window and door. He fired two shots at the places he thought the crawling gunmen would occupy before the final rush through the gate. And then he heard a renewal of a noise heard earlier, and he knew that the attack was about to develop in another direction. The cart had been withdrawn from the neighbouring copse and brought to the scene of the action.

Near it he could see Captain Verleigh and two or three of the men, although they were partially in cover.

How would they use the cart? Jim wondered. Perhaps they would run it down the hill with men laid flat in the back of it, and thus seek to get a formidable strike force close up to the house without casualties.

The sight of the vehicle gave him a deep sense of foreboding. For the first time since his brother and Vance had moved out, he became seriously apprehensive, and wondered just how long he ought to wait before attempting to safeguard his own life.

Bareheaded, he walked through to the rear of the building. He saw nothing of the escapers because the next development demanded his attention. A bullet came through a window from the stable on the low side, missing his head by the width of his finger. He sank to the ground with his heart thumping really hard.

One of the vicious trio had almost finished him then. Did they know, he wondered, that he was still alive within, and shooting against them? Or did they think the moving body was Vance or Big Sandy? He crept towards the window with his own query unanswered. Two bullets were sent into the building from which the latest attack had come. He knew then that he could not risk a rush out by the back door.

Almost certainly, he would be cut down by the gunman in the stable. He recollected with what cunning Prescott had moved across his flank earlier in the advance. The stable was occupied, now, the building on the other side might also hide a gunman; which meant that his time was seriously short now.

He blundered back into the front

room and tripped over the rug which had covered the trap. A bullet missed him which would have hit his shoulder, had he not stumbled. He peered anxiously through the window aperture and saw that men were guiding the cart down the hill. They were steering it backwards, using the shafts in order to do so.

It appeared to be loaded, but not with men. Bales and boxes were stacked in the interior, and that seemed to indicate a different sort of strike from the one Jim visualised.

His scalp crawled, and he had a feeling that fire was in some way to be used. The tinkling of glass signified an enemy on the other side, but he stayed where he was, rooted by the sight of the cart coming down the slope. Those men manœuvring it kept it clear of the trees and the boulders big enough to overturn it, or put it off-course. The last thirty yards or so before the gate were clear and sloped enough for the cart to plunge down it without a human escort.

He had the fear of fire known to man since primeval times. His fingers fumbled rather badly as he reloaded. Another pane of glass went . . . and with it he lost any desire to hurl himself out of the rear door and race for the creek.

He had to die Vance's death, or think of something new. Only the cellar opening appeared to provide any sort of alternative. Could he use it successfully, or would he, in secreting himself down there, deliver himself up to the stockman's army as a live prisoner who had changed sides?

He found a spy-glass and trained it on the cart and the men who were steering it. Within minutes he would know what they were up to. An ominous falling off in gunshots seemed to underline his summing up of the situation. The next fusillade, he felt sure, would precipitate the rush, but it was slow in coming.

★　★　★

Red Storme was as breathless as his struggling sorrel as he urged it out of the creek on the troubled side. Once clear of the water, it set its legs a little way apart and shook itself rather vigorously.

Mindful of the effort it had made, and his having brought it back into the conflict, Red leaned forward and fondly patted the white blaze on its head. It responded with a faint whinney, and turned its neck, as though wondering what he could ask of it next.

The lull was still on. Red did not like the silence. There was no evidence whatever to suggest that Jim had already left the shack and his ears had made it quite clear as he recrossed the water that the attackers were close on either hand; probably in the ranch outbuildings, too.

Instead of dashing back to the house, he manœuvred the sorrel on to a high knoll and there pulled out his glass, using it expertly on either side of the buildings. Within a minute, the rolling cart took his eye. His mouth opened of its own volition, and he trembled for the brother he had left behind. A half strangled cry came from his lips. He witnessed a man crawling into the cart and igniting a fuse which spluttered. *Dynamite!* And for extra measure, the torch was then tossed into the hay and bales, to make sure the explosion took place.

Out came the torch wielder to be pushed to the back by those who were setting the cart on its collision course. Ominously, no gunshots came from the ranch house. The men heaved, the cart started to roll down the hill. For a few moments, it looked as if it might foul the gate posts, but some small and unseen boulder bounced it in the right direction and sent it through the opened gate without touching the sides.

Men cheered viciously as it careered on its way across the yard, heading directly for the front of the building. Red thought: *If Jim is alive now, he'll be dead in a minute . . .*

He shook in the saddle, disturbing the sorrel and wondering if his eyes would ever function again after witnessing the inevitable explosion. The burning cart was out of his view now, and all he could do was dryly count the seconds until the cart hit the house, or the dynamite wad went up.

When the explosion came, it topped anything he expected.

The first thing he knew was when the ground shook and vibrated under him. The house roof appeared to develop a fringe of flame, but within a minute that disappeared. The walls were blown outwards by the force of the blast, and only a rear building prevented Red from seeing the total destruction of the shack in which he had spent all his spare time for almost a year and a half. Without knowing quite why, he dismounted. From the shelter of trees, he watched, and presently he climbed a tree and took a look from a higher altitude. The house, he felt sure, had been flattened. Burning where it had stood were scraps of furniture, and directly on the other side of it the burning cart was lighting up the countryside like a beacon, even in daylight.

Oddly enough, the fire had otherwise spread to the outbuildings on either side. The Vance homestead appeared to be a write-off, and with it the younger of the Storme brothers. Red climbed down again, experiencing a feeling of sickness which had nothing to do with vomiting, and one which would not leave him in a hurry.

He was faced with making a big decision. If he went back and sold his life dearly to the invaders, he would probably draw them after Paul Vance, who was not very far on the other side of the water and still weak. Now, he had to assume that Jim was dead, having failed to get clear of the house before the great holocaust. That being so, his duty clearly lay in helping Paul Vance to escape a similar fate.

For five minutes, he hovered amid

the trees near to the creek, waiting, and hoping against hope that Jim might crawl out of the nearest cover and greet him. But that did not happen, and finally he steeled himself to backtrack across the creek without having fired a single supporting shot.

8

The flooring of the ranch house smouldered. So did the rug which had partially concealed the cellar trapdoor. The two outbuildings on either side gushed smoke and flames, making the whole area a very chancy and unpleasant place to be in.

Captain Verleigh came as far as the gate, and permitted any of his men who wanted to go beyond it. Those who ventured forward, did so with their bandannas tightly stretched across their faces and dampened to prevent their being burned. They had strict instructions to look for and to find the bodies of the men who had defended the house.

Meldrum, Bracknell and Prescott were, of course, the first men to stand on the smouldering timbers and look around for the two defenders and Jim

Storme. They drew a total blank and went over the area again before the men who had manœuvred the cart moved in to cramp their style.

Bracknell was talkative. Meldrum said little. Prescott almost choked on the smoke when he tried to give his view. Slim waved his arms about, miming how the walls had been blown out, and giving that as his explanation for the lack of bodies. Any force which would demolish a house of four rooms, would make short work of a human or two.

The hot air in Meldrum's lungs began to hurt him. He gestured for his partners to move out with him. From a slightly greater distance, they observed as much as they could of the buildings on either side. The stable, which Meldrum had occupied earlier, was almost consumed. Moreover, he felt that he would have known if a body had been hurled against it while he was in there. Doc Prescott felt the same about the barn on the other side. Bracknell linked an arm in each of theirs and drew them back towards the cart.

There, they were confronted by Captain Verleigh, who looked anything but pleased.

'Well?' he demanded, his teeth almost clenched as he talked.

'No signs of bodies, Captain,' Meldrum explained. 'I don't think you expected any, did you? I mean, not after that explosion!'

'Bodies, of course I expected bodies, an' not charred ones, either! I wanted corpses which could be strung up an' left for the other rustlers to see, so they'd know what to expect if they still stood out against us! Don't you know we'll have to be movin' off soon, in case the sheriff gets this way with a posse? Have you searched *all* the outhouses?'

Slim Meldrum was quite a bit rattled by the Captain's tone and manner, particularly as the leader was looking mostly at him as he said his hostile words. 'We've seen all except one shack, an' that ain't likely to have a corpse in it. Still, since you're so fussy about bodies we'll take a look!'

'Maybe you'll let us know if a posse turns up while we're still lookin'?' Doc Prescott added, showing his nerve.

Verleigh turned his back on them. The possibility of a counter-attack was quite a possibility, and none knew it more than he. Another detail had gone wrong with his scheme. He had fully intended to exhibit bodies before he withdrew with his force to strike in another place.

Now, the shaken rustlers and their sympathisers would come crawling over Vance's ground without any clear idea as to what had happened to the association's first victim. Verleigh spat on the ground. He lit and smoked a cheroot for a few moments and then mashed it under his heel. Meldrum and the others were still not back. He undid the top button of his buckskin jacket and strode back up the hill.

The heat affected him more than most. He had time to wonder whether the fellow Storme had been a potential turncoat, and whether — as Meldrum suggested — he had died as he entered the house. Undoubtedly, the fellow was dead now, but it would have been interesting to know whether he died by a rustler's bullet or by dynamite.

★   ★   ★

For upwards of a minute, directly after searching the fourth building, Dixie Bracknell stood squarely in the middle of the trapdoor which covered the ventilated cellar. He might have taken a greater interest in the solid wooden cover had not the soles of his boots started to smoke at that instant. He backed off hurriedly, snorting through his broken nose and saying things about Captain Verleigh which might have greatly worsened the leader's opinion of him, had his words been audible.

Meldrum beckoned to him. He rejoined Slim at once. 'Cut it out, Dixie,' the other ordered. He pulled off his bandanna, mopped himself with it, and fingered some of the old smallpox marks on his face.

Prescott appeared beside them. 'Here, Dixie, take a swig at this flask. Only don't overdo it, because you know what you're like if you get a teaspoonful too much!'

Bracknell grabbed the flask, made as if to strike Prescott with it and then thought better of it. He emptied the air out of his mouth and took as big a swig of the whisky as he could do without drawing attention to himself. He set his teeth as the raw spirit ran down his gullet, and when the others were using the flask, he remarked to the world in general: 'Doggone me, if I'd had the chance to salivate that Storme, I'd be feelin' a whole lot better right now!'

⋆   ⋆   ⋆

Jim Storme was in the bottom of the cellar, reclining on his back on the rug, and breathing almost as badly as a landed fish sucks for water. He felt as if his head had swelled inside the hat. His whole body was wet with perspiration, and his lungs felt as though hot needles were pressing into them. And yet he knew that one, at least, of his ventilators was still working.

The trap above his head appeared to be expanding and contracting. He knew that it was not doing so, and yet most likely it was on fire on its upper side. The dynamite explosion had badly shaken his nerves and two or three minutes had gone by before he was able to rid himself of the idea that all the earth around him had to come in upon him and entomb him.

Since then, his morale was a little higher; but not much. He thought he had a great chance of avoiding the killers, but that he was likely to die of slow suffocation down his cellar. Even if he wanted to, he could scarcely avoid it because the quality of the air in the place had rendered him weak, and any exertion would undoubtedly hasten his untimely end. He closed his eyes, and tried to think of Red and Paul riding safely into the arms of a waiting posse, which only needed directions in order to avenge and drive the invaders out of Jackson County.

His eyes stayed shut, but his chest continued to work with an effort.

★ ★ ★

Meanwhile, Captain Verleigh became more angry and considerably more impatient. One of his scouts had heard noises which he thought might have been distant hoofbeats, and that could have meant a sudden arrival in the area of the peace officers and their deputised men.

Verleigh had the horses run down the slope. He shouted to his men to mount up, and when they were all in the saddle, he called out a few names and suggested that before they moved on they should scour the ground between the burning buildings and the creek.

Meldrum's party and those who had had charge of the cart were out of sorts with the leader. They hung back and allowed others to move on and search for the elusive bodies.

★ ★ ★

Some time earlier, Red had got as far as the creek, but then he had been unable to go through with his plan and cross it, owing to the lack of knowledge about Jim's fate. He had hovered about on the near bank and wondered if there was any possible chance of survival. His mind had been tormented by flashbacks to earlier episodes in the lives of the brothers. Things which neither of them could have forgotten easily.

Red kept telling himself that Paul would be all right in the dry gully which hid him on the far side of the creek. And yet Paul had been feverish when he left him, and far from his normal belligerent self.

Red was still fretting over his own

seeming ineffectiveness when Verleigh and the majority of his riders started to head towards the creek to water their mounts. Almost too late, Red heard them, and at last was able to get away from the bank which had held him.

He waited just long enough to know that a sizable body of riders was moving towards him, and then he acted. First he drew off his boots, and then he slackened the saddle girth, a thing which he had neglected to do earlier, and urged his mount into the water.

Red was a strong swimmer. He hoisted his boots and weapons well up on the sorrel's neck, and entered the water ahead of it. In the event that the animal was spotted before the crossing was completed, he had no intention of being bowled out of the saddle.

Man and horse made steady progress, and none of those who followed had any idea that a potential victim, a man worth fifty dollars dead, was slipping away from them.

★ ★ ★

Two pairs and a single rider answered the call to prowl around and search while the rest saw to the needs of their horses and acted as lookouts. The two pairs zigzagged back and forth over the near side of the creek, and one of them became excited when he discovered signs of a horse having recently entered the water.

Verleigh was becoming almost as disinterested as his men by then. He nodded and muttered over the sign, but showed no particular enthusiasm. On the other hand, he did not recall the solitary rider, Arizona Jake, who by that time had his pinto some twenty yards away from the bank.

Jake glanced back, saw that his move was approved and urged his horse to a greater speed. He emerged on the further bank and glanced down at the tracks left by horses entering and re-entering the water. There was no further sign up or down the creek, and he decided to follow his own inclinations. He plodded towards the north, moved into the nearest timber stand, and slipped out of leather. He had seen enough to believe there was still a chance of collecting fifty dollars, or even more.

Somebody had crossed quite recently. What he was not sure about was whether one of the riders was still on the ranch side or not.

Further inland from the creek, a few dozen head of cattle bawled about the smoke around the home buildings. Jake removed his spurs and walked on, horseless, carrying only his weapons. He was a markedly thin man of about thirty-six years with bloodshot eyes. The skin of his face had been darkened by unsightly powder burns, some of which he managed to hide with his black sideburns.

His scars had made him a solitary, withdrawn man, sufficiently maladjusted to be almost permanently against society. He kept walking for ten minutes. The strong growth of cactus and shrubs almost precipitated him into the narrow gully without his having seen it. He stepped down into it, re-orientated himself with the creek and the home buildings of the Vance spread and finally raised his sparse brows.

Very slowly and cautiously, he began to make his way down the gully which increased in depth as it meandered towards the creek again. Soon, he was on hands and knees. Fifteen minutes slow and arduous travel in this manner brought him in sight of his prize.

Paul Vance was stretched out on his back with his eyes closed, breathing rather heavily and obviously shaken by some sort of illness. He also was wounded, as a cloth around his left shoulder showed.

Arizona became still, as Vance sensed his presence.

'You been away a long time, Red. Did you find your brother all right?'

Jake moved nearer, two quick paces, and then stopped.

'You there, Red?' Vance complained. 'I may be feverish, but I can still take bad news if that's what you've brought! Will you tell me what's been happenin' or do I have to crawl over an' look for myself? Red?'

'All right, all right, calm down, Vance.'

Jake's words had the opposite effect, but the crawling man was within striking distance. He had his right arm raised with a knife in it when Vance rolled away to one side. But the arm came down, just the same, and the blade was buried in the wounded man's back instead of his breast. Vance threshed about for almost half a minute, and then lay still.

Arizona took a little longer, removing his blade rather leisurely and wondering about the titbit of intelligence he had heard from the dead man's lips. A man named Red had gone off to try and bring back his brother. But there was no mention of a brother at the ranch. Perhaps this Red was Big Sandy, and

Big Sandy had a brother. It seemed strange that Verleigh did not know about Sandy's brother. Perhaps he would be pleased to hear the information from Jake's lips.

Instead of standing up and calling to the rest of his party, Jake acted on a hunch and started to crawl down the rest of the gully. A hiding place which could turn up an escaper might just turn up another of the same ilk.

★   ★   ★

Jake's hunch was a good one. Red Storme was ahead of him down the gully and much nearer to the creek. Some ten minutes later, Red heard the crawler's approach. He thought it odd that Vance should be so much nearer to the creek than the place where he had left him; and yet a man in the grip of fever might do all manner of unlikely things.

Red waited another five minutes, and then decided to try out the approaching man. He filled his lungs for a whisper that had to carry. Just before he called the name, he was moved to act with great caution. He put off the call for a few seconds, and took time out to hoist his body above the rim of the gully.

'Paul? Is that you?'

'Sure, keep comin' will you? I got a little anxious back there on my own, an' my shoulder aches.'

'Stay where you are, Paul,' Red advised.

The voice he had heard might have been that of Vance, except that the fever had made the rancher talk thickly. A man would scarcely have thrown off the troublesome fever in so short a time. Red, accordingly, made a detour. He heard his name called once more, but ignored it.

Just when the doubts were building up in him again, he blundered into the pinto, and knew that his fears were not imaginary. He made use of the animal to get to the place where he had left Paul. The shock of finding him with a knife wound in his back was still with him as he hoisted the lifeless body and heaved it across the pinto.

Paul could not be left behind to be used as an exhibit by the marauders, no matter what the risks were. So thought Red at that juncture. But when he approached the creek again, upstream of the place where Arizona Jake had left the pinto, the sounds of many hostile horsemen crossing the water carried to his ears.

He glanced at the still form of his friend and decided that if he — Red — was to live to seek vengeance, they would have to part company, after all. He forced himself to slap the pinto across the rump, and sent it away from the approaching riders in the hope that it would walk as far as the Lazy K.

For his own safety, he hastened back to the creek, dived in, and swam it the other way, passing most of the distance under water, relying on his lungs to minimise the risk. A willow hid him until dark when he whistled up his sorrel and started to think about the future.

A moonless sky nerved him to make another trip across the water to recover his saddle, which he had removed and hidden some time earlier. His night probing, however, drew an accurate shot from a camp guard before he actually recovered the invaluable piece of leather, and he withdrew to a safe distance feeling extremely thankful that his skin was still intact.

9

Jim was actually unconscious for a short time in the bottom of the cellar which had saved him from the mighty blast of the dynamite. He was slow to regain consciousness, and when he did so, he had to breathe shallowly and wonder for a time what was his greatest potential danger.

Not far off, he could hear the splutter of bark burning, as it burst away from a tree trunk. But the sound of men was non-existent. The second of the two ventilation holes had ceased to show any signs of daylight, and that, to a trapped man, seemed very significant.

His first reaction was to think that the other end of the hole was blocked. He continued to believe this for quite a time.

The sides of his cellar had been well shored up by planks, but every now and again loose pieces of earth pattered down behind the boards, sounding like moving animals. Jim shuddered. Dirt and dust had formed thickly around the fold in his bandanna. A simple move of the head sent them coursing down his neck, inside his shirt.

He began to feel for the first time in his life the fear of enclosed spaces. Some time later, he panted as he moved up the steps towards the trap which he had come to think would never open to release him. Men, he had ceased to fear for the time being, as he believed that they had withdrawn; but he did not expect to get out into the open air which so short a time ago had been full of whining bullets.

The underside of the trap was hot to his gloved hand. He brought it away, and instead he applied the barrel of his Winchester to the board. To his surprise, it moved without undue pressure, and a small gap appeared. Smoke and small flying embers surged through the gap, and made him release his hold. He coughed and his eyes smarted afresh.

Almost in desperation, he renewed his assault upon the trap, and straightened with his head above ground level as it swung away and fell back upon its hinges with a resounding crack. Smoke and red embers swirled afresh, but the man who had emerged blinked them away in his keenness to study the immediate devastation.

The stable and the other near building were burned to the ground. Of the ranch house, there was little except the burning embers of the floor and a few odd metal shapes which suggested pots and pans. A little further off were metal hoops which had once been part of cart wheels, and bigger hoops which supported canvas over the rear of the vehicle.

The pump was dripping water. No attempt at all had been made to use the pump water to fight fire. It was a scene of almost total devastation. Jim staggered across to the pump and put his head under it. The water refreshed him, and was almost too much for him at first. He sluiced himself down slowly and carefully, and realised fully for the first time that it was dusk.

The battle for the homestead, and the destruction of the buildings had seen out the remaining hours of daylight. He seated himself upon a boulder still warm from the fire, and wondered what he ought to do.

He was tired and there were so many things he wanted to know which he could scarcely learn about until morning. His head drooped forward. He was feeling the reaction after all the pent-up excitement. Red, he figured, had got away with Vance. The invaders had moved on, and the protectors of the ordinary people had not this far arrived. Probably they had been scattered to start with, owing to minor attacks to the south-east of Sweetwater perpetrated by those who should have gunned the peace officers.

He yawned, and yawned again.

Only the need to see exactly how Paul Vance had fared kept Sheriff Amos Grant and the ten riders with him moving towards the Vance ranch after nightfall. Grant's mouth was set in a tight line for two reasons. One was an all-consuming anger about the way the big cattlemen had acted, and the other was because he felt weary.

Earlier in the day, he had split his group of riders with his chief deputy, Bart McGivern, and they had ridden in different directions. Bart had gone further north and east than the sheriff. The latter had looked over the burnt-out remains of the Drummond place, and failed to find any sign of the men who had fired it.

The afternoon had given way to evening when they had the first intimation that all was not well along the small ranchers' creek. Even after receiving a warning, Grant had not hurried unduly because he had anticipated the attack being made against Dick Tollman's Lazy K. He had secret knowledge that the Lazy K was well defended and that any strike against that small ranch, or any of its immediate neighbours, would result in the invaders being repulsed at great cost.

Amos was annoyed with himself. Verleigh's change of plans had rendered him helpless again. He had ridden for the last mile or two hearing the quiet taunts and criticism of the men who rode behind him. Several of them had wanted to make a better pace after leaving Drummond's homestead, but he had dissuaded them, and now they were blaming him for having arrived so late in sight of the smoking ruins of Vance's tiny place.

There it lay, less than a quarter of a mile away from them, shrouded in smoke and occasional flickers of flame as the breeze stirred old embers.

'One think we can be sure of,' one rider remarked, 'if Paul Vance is down there, he'll be danglin' from the end of a rope, an' his man, Big Sandy, with him!'

Grant wanted to argue that they had probably been blasted to death when the house went up, but he knew that argument would get them nowhere. His tiredness weighed him down, and made it hard for him to make the last decisions for the day. He thought that if he had been in the pay of the invaders he could not have handled his men with less skill that day.

A sudden crack made them all keen again. It was a rifle shot fired on the far side of the creek.

'How about that, Sheriff?'

The voice was that of Hank Norton, a forty-year-old balding man with deep-set narrow eyes and an up-swept hat brim. Norton had been one of the loudest in criticism of the sheriff. Now he kneed his mount and rode forward to the peace officer's side.

'Some activity down on the other side,' Grant replied calmly.

'Well? Are we goin' across to see if

Vance is still alive, or do we dawdle down there an' give him a call in an hour or so?'

Norton's voice had hardened as he went on. He was so close to the sheriff that they could see one another's faces quite clearly. Grant, in spite of his tiredness, stared the other down without apparent effort.

'Norton, if ever I swear in a posse again, you won't be in it. You talk too much, an' your emotions show through your words. If I wasn't interested in the small men in these parts, I'd be at home now, snorin' in my bed! Nobody told me I was forced to do otherwise! I'm here because I think this is my duty! I'm not the commander of Fort Lerwick, nor the Governor of this state! All I represent is Jackson County, an' the way my nerves are playin' me up at the moment, I'm jest as likely to shoot you as any hired gun slinger who cuts across my path! Hold it!'

Norton had been about to turn his horse and move away in a huff. He stayed where he was, but purposely avoided Grant's eyes from then on.

'You can tell the other boys that we are goin' down to Vance's place. I don't want a headlong rush down the slope for obvious reasons. An' when we hit the ranch, back off an' keep quiet. These sidewinders we're dealin' with are cunnin' enough to have laid another trap for the likes of us!'

Grant waited a minute. In that time, he wondered how Bart had made out. Obviously, there was a small party of invaders busy further north and east than Drummond's place, but they were mobile enough to take a lot of finding.

While he was still unhappily conjecturing, the riders bunched behind him, and a new voice spoke out.

'Sheriff, we want you to know that we think you must be good an' tired, an' that goes for all of us. You do things the way you planned them, only make sure we get any changes of instruction in a clear voice.'

Grant raised his hand without looking back. He touched his gelding's flanks with the rowels and started down the hill. Soon they were through the paddock gate and standing their horses in a tight crescent in front of the razed ranch. Grant sighed. Without thinking very much why he did it, he lifted his hat. The others at once did the same.

They backed off and looked about, studying the nearest trees and hoping that they would not find corpses dangling from them. Several minutes went by while they looked. Eventually all the riders came back and reported that they had found nothing.

Grant hated saying: 'Don't build up your hopes. Paul Vance wasn't the kind of man to withdraw without a struggle, an' dynamite's been used here.'

Norton, urging his mount further forward than the rest, noticed the trapdoor which was still open. He waved his hat at it.

'I ain't so sure you need to be all that

pessimistic, Sheriff,' he began. 'Somebody's sheltered here, an' we heard that shot a while back! Could be Vance *did* survive!'

'I never ruled out such a possibility,' Grant retorted. 'Don't build up is all I said. Now, if you're ready, I think we ought to mosey forward as far as the creek, afore we turn in for the night!'

Norton whistled through his teeth.

'Save it!' Grant warned.

The horses picked their way daintily through the debris and emerged on the other side, clearly relieved to move away from the smell of burning timber. Some twenty yards past the buildings, Grant snapped his fingers. He had instant attention from the others, who were more intent on taking instructions when the possibility of action loomed up.

Half of them went to the right of the sheriff, and the rest moved away on his left. He swung out of leather and stood by his horse's head, while others did the same and focused their tired eyes on what he had already seen. A man was kneeling by the waters of the creek on the near side. He did not appear to have noticed their approach. In fact, so still was his figure that he might have been asleep.

Weapons blossomed in the hands of the riders who had done too much riding and seen no action. Fifteen yards from the figure, Grant signalled for them to pause. They did so, and he went forward alone. Although the approach was a quiet one, something must have gone through to the sleeping man's brain. He made the slightest move, and his tired body tilted over.

Grant stepped to his side and prodded him with a Colt. Jim Storme gasped, rocked his weary head and looked up into the hard, vengeful face above him. He found it hard to take his gaze away from Grant's eyes, even in the semi-gloom, but presently the star pinned to the black vest drew his attention.

Jim started to laugh rather weakly. He made an effort and rose to his feet, topping the sheriff by a few inches. Grant kept the Colt where it was, sticking into Jim's side.

'Thank goodness you made it, Sheriff.' Jim sounded relieved. 'For your information, I'm Jim Storme. My brother, Red, was in the ranch back there with Paul Vance when the attack developed.'

Norton led the surge forward of the others. 'Vance never had no hired help other than that Big Sandy, Sheriff! I know this for a fact! This man is a stranger! I'd say he's one of the hired guns, an' somehow he's lost his hoss!'

Norton's latest outburst was niggling the lawman, but he nevertheless asked a question while Jim was still way back on the defensive.

'What did you do with your hoss, Storme?'

Jim's eyes went from one face to the other. He realised then and there that if he was too frank with these self-appointed killers working for the peace officer he would scarcely be believed. Red wasn't here to back him now. Neither was Vance, and this party did not appear to have been in touch with either, otherwise they would have been told to look out for him.

'I was in the cellar under the shack when the cart loaded with dynamite blew up on impact. I was down there for hours. I couldn't tell you what happened directly after that. All I know is that my brother an' Vance, who was wounded, lit out some little time before the invaders closed in. Does that satisfy you, Sheriff?'

Norton filled his lungs to say that it did not, but Grant reached out with his free hand and gripped the deputy's shoulder. Norton remained silent.

Speaking out of the side of his mouth, Grant remarked: 'The next hombre who sounds off loudly at the mouth will be pistol-whipped by me, an' that's a promise.' He changed the tone of his voice and went on: 'About that shot, a short while back, mister.

Did you hear it?'

'Sure, I heard it. I got as far as the creek after it sounded off, but then my energy ran out on me. I fell asleep where you found me.' In an awkward silence, he added: 'I don't know who fired the shot. The imagination plays tricks. I like to think it was one of the invaders' guards shootin' at shadows. It didn't have to mean they had a human target.'

Sheriff Grant hustled Jim back through the bunched groups of his men. 'I'm keepin' you close with us until daylight, young fellow. We'll make camp right here, an' you'll be positioned on the creek side of us. If you happen to be on the other side, you'll be the first to absorb bullets in the event of an attack from that quarter.'

Jim took this announcement quite calmly. He allowed them to truss his wrists and ankles, but before Grant finally moved away, he had a question to ask.

'Sheriff, if you really knew whether

Vance an' my brother had survived, you'd tell me, wouldn't you?'

'I believe I would at that, young fellow.' Grant was scratching at his chin beard as though he could tear it off. He lurched away with his slight limp exaggerated. When the camp was established, Norton and one other man wanted to question the sheriff's policy about the supposed enemy camp on the other side of the water. He told them quite patiently that an attack of that sort, mounted with tired men against a superior enemy with night guards, was like asking for annihilation.

Neither Norton nor his sympathiser had encountered the word 'annihilation' before, but they guessed at its meaning and took time out to inform the rest of the group before turning in. The first two guards had difficulty in keeping their eyes open for their allotted span, but the night passed uneventfully.

10

In spite of his aches and pains and a raging thirst which made the back of his throat dry and raw, Jim did not rouse himself at all easily the following day. His eyelids felt as though they were made of lead. He had problems, and he knew it. He decided to let matters stay the way they were until the sheriff made some decisions.

A man who took short steps came close to him shortly after the guards had roused the whole party. The toe of a boot came quite near to his ribs. Its very next move would have to be against his person, but before this could happen the only familiar voice intervened.

'Let him alone!'

Grant's voice, which was curt and salty at the best of times, had an added penetration at that early hour of the morning. The wearer of the boot, Hank

Norton, sniffed and backed off. He retreated rather slowly and was glad that his intended victim had not witnessed what happened.

The fire was built up while lookouts ranged themselves along the near bank of the creek, and other men back-tracked to the ranch to find non-existent clues to the fate of the owner.

Norton and another were given special permission to scout beyond the creek before the fried breakfast was consumed. They left with their jaws still working. Grant, noticeably, turned his back on them and gave his full attention to the rashers of bacon which were a staple part of his early diet.

Even the smell of the food did not immediately rouse Jim. He was still only half awake when footsteps approached him again, and a voice which he had not heard for a long time made a pronouncement.

'Sure enough, Amos, this is my cousin, Jim Storme. He looks to have had a rough time since I saw him last, but I couldn't be mistaken.'

Bart McGivern knelt beside the trussed man and began to fumble with the wrist cords. Sheriff Grant went down on his knees, too.

'Are you sure you know all you need to know about your cousin, Bart? I mean, well, in ordinary circumstances I'd take your say-so about a fellow like this. But we're livin' in strange, unholy times. Can you say beyond doubt that he's trustworthy?'

Before McGivern could answer, Jim rolled to one side. His dry and cracked lips formed into a smile as he winked his eyes for the first time.

'Hell an' tarnation, Bart, you boys who came to Wyomin' sure did end up in the thick of things! You wearin' a badge, too?'

McGivern finished tinkering with the cords and as soon as Jim could manage it, he thrust forward his right hand and shook that of his cousin quite warmly. Soon, his ankles were free, too, and he was walking around rather gingerly with a mug of coffee in his hand.

When they were a few yards out of earshot of the others, he confided in the star toters. Nodding to Bart, he said: 'The sheriff, here, was right to be suspicious of me last night, Bart. As a matter of fact, I allowed myself to be fooled into joinin' that stockmen's outfit. A fellow over in Idaho told me a pack of lies when he knew I was comin' this way to link up with Red an' you. I thought they wanted straightforward cowpunchers until I got mixed up with the hired guns.

'Imagine my surprise when all this developed.'

Bart asked: 'Did you know they were goin' against Vance, an' that Red was in there with him?'

'I knew it belonged to a man named Vance, but I couldn't back out at that stage. I'd grumbled a time or two, an' certain guns, namely one Slim Meldrum an' his sidekicks, were seekin' a chance to have me salivated.'

'If things were goin' against you, how

did you get into the place like you claim you did?' Grant wanted to know.

'Captain Verleigh wanted four men to spearhead the attack. Meldrum, Bracknell an' Prescott volunteered an' insisted on me bein' the fourth. There was a fifty dollar bonus for anyone killed who was on Dodge's black list, so I was suspicious of their motives in choosing me.'

'You thought you might be shot in the back, perhaps,' Bart suggested.

'I very nearly was,' Jim put in excitedly.

'But if you were ahead of the other hostile guns, how did you get the defenders to trust you?' Grant asked.

'I caught sight of Red when he ducked out to get water. Then I remembered an old gun signal we used to use when we were kids. A rifle shot followed by two revolver shots. He picked it out, an' I fell into the house. Shortly after that, they fired three shots, as though I'd been killed on arrival.'

The peace officers were looking

pleased and satisfied with this explanation, but they were still not fully in the picture.

'When they sent that go-devil, the dynamited cart, against the buildin', did they think you dead, or did they want you dead with the others?' Grant probed pointedly.

Jim looked baffled. 'I suppose it could have been either. I don't think the leader trusted me, an' I'm sure those Texas killers talked against me, anyways. I wish I knew how Red an' Vance had fared, though.'

He went on to outline all he knew about the late developments of the previous day, and by the time he was through answering questions, Hank Norton was on his way back across the creek with the latest news from his scouting expedition.

'We located the place where a large number of riders spent the night, Sheriff,' he called, from ten yards out, 'but they ain't there now an' they left nothin' by way of identification. No

149

bodies about, either.'

Jim sighed with relief, and so did Bart, who was just as concerned. The breakfast meal was prolonged for Jim's benefit. While he ate, Bart backtracked and brought along the men who had ridden in the second posse. They, too, were pretty played out by their tour of the previous day, but their arrival put a certain amount of heart into the sheriff's men because they had fired a few hostile shots and had something to talk about.

Bart's party had rather luckily happened upon six invading riders just when the latter were on the point of breaking camp and mounting up. No one had waited for orders to open fire. A ragged volley had hit the imported guns. One had been killed almost instantly, and his body had plunged down a deep gully where it had been left. Another had been wounded twice over, but he had managed to keep his seat and retain control of his horse.

Along with the other survivors he had

been chased determinedly, and in the early afternoon the survivors had been glad to cross the North Platte river and submerge themselves into broken ground from which they were most unlikely to emerge again as a fighting unit. Hence the return of Bart's posse in time to link up with the sheriff's group.

When the parlaying was at an end, and Bart's party had been absorbed with the other, Jim thought he was well enough established with the group to ask a few questions.

'Bart, if you come across one of the invaders forkin' a big dun hoss with a black mane an' tail, don't shoot it, 'cause it's mine. Keep it for me, will you, if you come across it?'

Bart made the obvious promise.

'I started out badly in this campaign,' Jim admitted. 'Perhaps you, Sheriff, could suggest some way in which I could act to even things up a little.'

Grant shrugged, and glanced at Bart, who had just mounted, but the latter had nothing to suggest. 'If he can't bear to come along with us after the main body of the army, the only thing we could do is use him as a messenger.'

Jim looked up from a spindly claybank, which had been loaned to him. 'How would it be if I managed to bring in the army, Sheriff?'

Grant rolled himself a smoke and patiently explained the position. Jim took it all in, and said that he still wanted to have a try at bringing in the cavalry from Fort Lerwick.

'You won't get them to come along without the say-so of the governor, Jim,' Grant replied, 'but if you're determined to go the C.O.'s name is Major Brentford. He's noted in the county, but the governor is a known friend of his, so don't expect to do wonders. If you do manage to get a sympathetic hearin', though, impress upon the C.O. the need for instant action! Otherwise there's little hope for a lot of the local people.'

Jim accepted the advice and tried to

think of something to say to Bart before parting company. 'I know you're goin' after the main body of the enemy, Bart, but keep a lookout for Red an' Paul, won't you?'

'We won't overlook isolated friends, Jim,' Grant said, butting in, 'an' mind how you go yourself, because we don't know where the invaders are headin' right now. They might have decided to give the Lazy K a wide berth after all that's happened.'

Grant was showing impatience at last. He took his men along the near bank of the creek, while Jim urged his borrowed claybank into the creek waters, taking the nearest direction to Fort Lerwick. Soon, the waving and the calling of farewells were over, and he was on his own, riding on what was perhaps a fool's errand which would take him out of the firing line.

With these sort of thoughts in his head, he pushed the claybank hard until about one in the afternoon. After resting for an hour, he moved on again.

Late in the afternoon, he had a stroke of luck. Fort Lerwick was some distance away, but he came upon a troop of horse doing manœuvres down the side of a hogsback ridge.

A strict young lieutenant was training his squad in putting their mounts to a down slope. Every ten yards they had to pull up, draw their carbines and take aim at an imaginary enemy in the defile on the low ground.

Jim waited patiently for them to come down. He had the weapons trained on him no fewer than five times before the officer expressed himself satisfied with the way the drill had been carried out and permitted the men a ten-minute break at the bottom.

Jim walked the claybank towards him as he dismounted from a blowing grey stallion. 'That's a good lookin' hoss you have there, sir,' the Texan observed with a grin.

He knew that his face bore several small burn marks from the clashes of the previous day, but that was no excuse for the sneering look which spread across the features of the arrogant young man. Lieutenant Peter Radwell, aged twenty-four, was a native of New England. He could never quite get over the fact that he had no war service to his credit, and he therefore ran his troop strictly by the book, and particularly so on manoeuvres.

Jim studied the facial expression, taking in the bluish lantern jaw. He began to have doubts whether this fellow would give him a sympathetic hearing. The officer turned away, and made a big thing out of slackening his saddle.

'Do you have any special interest in the United States cavalry, mister?'

'As a matter of fact, I have. I'm on my way to Fort Lerwick with a message from the sheriff of Jackson County. I hope to contact the Commanding Officer without delay.'

'I'm afraid he won't want to see you unless the business is of a military nature. But in any case, the C.O. is not at the fort. He's up country on a huntin' expedition.'

This last piece of information jolted Jim, but he set his lips in a firm line when he realised the lieutenant was trying to discourage him. 'My business is important enough to merit immediate attention. It concerns an invasion of Jackson County by hired guns. Several people have died already, to my certain knowledge. Failin' the C.O. I'll have to talk to his deputy.'

The lieutenant made another attempt to freeze Jim out, but he failed. Veteran Sergeant John Smith, a man in his forties with spiky grey hair, managed to have a short conversation with Jim before the officer gave the word to fall in again.

When he had heard the first true details about the invasion, the N.C.O. apologised for having little to say which could promote confidence.

'We're headed back for the fort tonight. The lieutenant likes to sleep in his bed, even if it's only for a few hours.

But the actin' C.O. won't be much of an improvement on Radwell, so don't be too hopeful. O' course, if he happens to fall down an' break 'is neck on the way back, I could turn the troop round an' 'ave them in action by early tomorrow.'

Radwell was snappy with his sergeant. When they went off in a neat file, they were hurried back towards base at a good speed. If they hoped to shake off the lone civilian, however, they were disappointed. Jim was well up with them when they went through the gate in the defensive wall.

A corporal on guard insisted that Captain Robb could not be disturbed until the next day, but Jim was not having any. He made his way towards the officers' quarters, and insisted that they would have to shoot him to stop him. In that way, he received an interview in the C.O.'s office at a very late hour. Captain Robb, dressed for a dinner, and smoking a cigar, interviewed him from the depths of the commanding officer's chair.

Jim removed his hat. 'My name is Storme, sir. I bring a message from Amos Grant, the sheriff of Jackson County. I have to tell you that a small army of mercenaries is killin' an' pillagin', burnin' down ranches an' so on in the southern party of the county. Military aid is needed at once to safeguard the civilian population. I hope you'll be able to see your way to sendin' troops to the sheriff's aid without delay.'

Robb removed his cigar and chuckled.

'Young man, the military cannot be turned out to help civilians without a directive from the governor.'

Robb glanced across at a mirror on the other side of the room. He seemed to admire his suave reflection, his blue eyes, and the distinguished-looking style of his greying hair.

'I believe the governor is indisposed,' Jim retorted glibly.

Robb frowned. 'The governor's deputy is in charge. My commanding officer, who is away hunting at this time, was in communication with the governor's office not long ago. We have another slant on this mercenary invasion, as you call it. We have it on the very best authority that the Wyoming stockmen are acting well within the limits of the law. You have been misinformed, sir.'

Robb rose to his feet. At that juncture, Jim's self-possession failed him. 'It is you who are misinformed. I came into Wyoming with this — this uncouth band of killers, so *I* know. It seems to me there's a conspiracy to keep out the soldiers, an' you, Captain, appear to be a party to it.'

Robb turned to leave the room by the other door. He flicked ash from his cigar to the floor with an elegant hand.

He remarked: 'Your manners are bad, even for a cowboy, but then we must not expect too much. You'll be given a bed for the night, of course, if you can be civil to the corporal of the guard. Tomorrow you must leave. This is no place for civilians, believe me.'

Jim was still fuming when Sergeant Smith, the man who had been out with Radwell's detail, helped him to make up a bunk in a store beyond the men's quarters.

'It's true Major Brentford is out huntin', an' I'll tell you somethin' not many folks know around here. The important person he has with him is the governor, 'imself. Not Mister Cy Beaumont, but 'is boss, George Thompson. Now, if you could get the Major an' Thompson to listen to you, all this would be changed. The Governor hasn't a lot of time for cattle barons, an' the Major is one of the fairest-minded men in the army.'

'Where would I look if I sought them while they were out huntin', sergeant?'

Smith lowered his voice to a whisper, but he had the necessary information.

11

Skinny Todd lived on the nearest homestead to the Vance place on the other side of the creek. The Lazy K, which had been hurriedly prepared to withstand a siege, lay some four miles to northward of Skinny's home.

Although he was sixty-one years of age, the bearded and somewhat unkempt settler had been along to help Tollman and the others prepare the defences of the Lazy K. Todd had annoyed his neighbours, however, by refusing to bring his wife and two adopted sons behind the prepared defences until the time of the present emergency was over.

Skinny had argued with the others. He pointed out that he was advanced in years, that he had only recently broken the habit of a lifetime, namely, that of prospecting. Now, he wanted to be on his own land with his own kin. If necessary, he would die there. His land was the only land he was prepared to fight for.

About eight o'clock on the morning after the Vance ranch was burned down, the pinto carrying the dead body of Paul Vance gradually approached the Todds' small territory. It started to crop grass beyond Skinny's fences, and it was Martha, the wife, who first saw it and identified the burden it carried.

She reached down a shotgun from the wall and trotted across to the fence gate, which she opened with some diffidence. Martha was nearly twenty years younger than her husband. She was hard of face, and sharp-tongued, but those who lived with her knew the warmness of her heart. Her brown hair was long and fixed in a bun at the back of her head. During the past year it had started to turn grey. Her breast heaved under a thin white blouse above a shiny, worn work shirt.

She knew Paul Vance, of course, and her imagination was not needed to tell her how he had died. His fatal wound was there for anyone to see. Martha was thinking about her own kin, and Skinny's bullheadedness. She knew his feelings better than anyone, but now she thought he had been foolish to turn down the comparative safety of the Lazy K ranch.

Vance had been a big tough individual, and so had Big Sandy, his man. They had gone under in the face of the invaders, and so could her old husband and the two boys. She glanced around sharply. There was no reason to think Vance's killers were anywhere close. The pinto horse was a stranger to her. She wondered how far away the nearest strangers were at that moment. It occurred to her that the corpse and horse might have been directed towards Skinny's place in an effort to draw out the family.

Her mouth dried out as one sinister plot after another occurred to her. Some three hundred yards to the northwest, Skinny straightened up from his digging and saw the strange horse and its load. She waved to him. He tossed down his fork and started towards the log shack.

Zack, the older of the two adopted boys, was working within fifty yards of Skinny. He called out, but was waved back to his work and told to stay away. At sixteen years of age, Zack had thick, curly fair hair, and his thin frame was gradually filling out through good food and steady exercise. His round, expressive brown eyes, showed anger. He figured that he was old enough to be treated as a man. Nevertheless, he picked up his tool and went on working.

Skinny's steps slowed as he came nearer to the gate and the corpse. He stopped with the horse between him and his wife, and tried to brush down his long hair with horny fingers.

He murmured: 'Paul? Paul Vance?'

Martha nodded. 'I don't know that we ought to let the boys see what's happened to him, Skinny.'

The horny hands massaged the old man's thighs. 'I know the way you feel, Martha, but they'll be men some day. Zack, back there, knows what's afoot already.'

'Let him stay where he is,' the wife replied fiercely. 'An' Little Abe don't have to know. He's over to that stream on the north side, figurin' to snare a jackrabbit.'

Skinny nodded in agreement. 'So we ought to get Paul offen this hoss an' into a position of more dignity, wife. Maybe you'll give me a hand?'

Martha walked the pinto round the back of the two buildings and helped her spouse to lower the limp form to the ground. They carried Vance's remains into the shed, put a cloth over him and left him there.

'What are we goin' to do with him?' the woman asked, as they paused outside.

The pinto wandered past them before Skinny answered. 'Some time soon I'll have to bury him. Not yet, though. Seein' his body like this takes a bit of gettin' used to. Besides, there'll be others might want to see him before he gets planted.'

Martha nodded. 'I'll make some coffee before you go back.'

Skinny took enough of the liquid along with him to slake Zack's thirst as well. He made heavy going of the walk to the digging place and spilled some of his coffee before he got the mug to his lips. Then Zack was crowding him, his eyes wide and fear lurking deep behind them.

'Who was that across the hoss' back? It was Paul Vance, wasn't it? I know, because they fired his place last night an' you've been expectin' trouble ever since! Do you still think you did the right thing by stayin' out here when the other men were takin' their kin along to be with the Lazy K crowd?'

This outburst overwhelmed Skinny, who was greatly upset over what had happened to Vance. 'All right, so if you think I was wrong you can take the mare an' go to Tollman's place right now. You hear me?'

'Of course you were right,' Zack retorted. 'Only Vance was a mighty fine fellow, an' it cuts me up to see him come in here like that on the back of a strange hoss, doggone it!'

Skinny sighed. He picked up his tool again, and Zack did the same. Side by side, they started to dig again. Gradually, Zack's pent-up anger started to diminish. Neither of them wanted to be the first to stop for a rest. They could not trust their emotions at that time.

An upthrust of earth came between them, and Zack put his more youthful shoulders into the earth on the rougher side, the one which was thick with bunch grass and overgrown sage.

★   ★   ★

Arizona Jake was within twenty feet of the shack and aiming to pat the cropping pinto before Martha was aware of his presence. She glanced through a window and noted the way in which the stranger behaved towards the animal.

At once, she sensed the worst. Jake had a hand on the horse's mane when she threw open the door and brought up the shotgun. The stranger's blood-shot eyes showed surprise when the muzzle of the gun was presented towards him. He brought up his right hand to his face, fingering his powder-darkened skin, and tickling his chin with the point of the knife which rested up his sleeve on the inside of his forearm.

'Now, missus, that surely ain't the way to treat a stranger, is it now? Particularly one who's lookin' for his runaway hoss, an' who finds it in your yard. So put up your gun an' act a little more friendly towards a wayfarer.'

Martha shook her head. 'Oh no, you don't, stranger! On account of the body draped across that hoss' back when it got here, an' because of what happened to the owner of the ranch across the water! You have hired gun written all over you an' I'm not aimin' to let you have your way with *my* kin!'

Jake shrugged. He removed his hand from the back of the pinto, and lowered the other one in a seemingly open-handed gesture. When the woman did not waver, the man glanced across towards the meadow and allowed his expression to alter as though he had learned something new, which had a bearing upon their meeting.

This was too much for Martha, who was worrying about Skinny and Zack. She glanced away, and in that instant Jake let fly the knife which was his favourite weapon. Martha took the blade full in the breast. She did not have the strength to shout a warning, and she fell back over her own threshold, dropping the gun as she did so.

Oddly enough, the shotgun did not go off. Jake strolled across to the shack, assured himself that Martha was already dead, and then recovered his blade, which he wiped on her skirt. He dragged her further indoors, rolled himself a smoke and walked out again, his mind on other things.

Perspiration was coursing through Skinny's beard when the soft voice called out to him and set his hackles rising.

'Hey, mister, can you direct me to the ranch of Paul Vance?'

The fork clattered off a stone. Skinny straightened up. 'If you want assistance come out into the open an' show yourself.'

His voice was scarcely louder than the other man's as he did not want to alarm Zack. A casual glance around showed him that Zack was now some fifty yards away and mostly hidden by the sage. The old man was very doubtful about the disembodied voice. He had no knowledge of what had happened to Martha back at the shack.

The voice taunted him. 'Are you sayin' you charge for information in these parts, or do you have to like a

170

man's face before you give it?'

Skinny muttered an oath. He covered the five yards distance to where his Henry lay in two short leaps. He had the gun almost to his shoulder when the two hidden weapons sounded off. Two rifle bullets ripped into him from different angles. One hit him in the head, and the other in the heart. He pivoted on his heels for a second or so, and then fell flat right where he had dug.

Slim Meldrum was the first to arrive. He was followed by Bracknell.

'You know, Dixie, if this ole coot had to be buried, we could do it right here, on account of him bein' a first-class sod buster. Sure is good at his work, wasn't he?'

Bracknell stepped carefully over to the corpse and studied the hole in the temple where his bullet had entered. He sniggered over Slim's comment and showed his appreciation by giving the other an admiring glance.

'Seems like the two of us will have to

share the fifty bonus offered for this old he-goat. I'd say he's Skinny Todd, for sure. That Arizona fellow has dealt with the wife. Do you think there'll be anyone else around, or will they have shipped the next generation up to the Lazy K?'

'I'd say we've about got the place to ourselves, Dixie, apart from the stiffs. But the countryside is ominously quiet at this moment. We can't afford to let up.' He lowered his voice, and whispered: 'Got any idea what Doc's playin' at?'

Bracknell murmured that he was no wiser. Between them they picked up Skinny's body and carried him with his legs trailing towards the buildings. They were almost there when poor Zack's patience gave out. He sprang after the killers of Skinny with an old army Colt in his fist. Unfortunately, he went quite close to the hideout of little Doc Prescott, who rose up out of nowhere and jabbed him hard in the ribs with his rifle barrel.

Zack gagged and dropped his weapon. He was led ignominiously towards the others with another revolver sticking in his back.

Arizona Jake permitted himself one of his rare smiles when he saw how the other three had fared. He casually trussed the shocked youth hand and foot and left him tied to the pommel of the pinto by his lariat.

Jake did not miss the wariness of the other three. Prescott, in particular, kept a careful eye on the surrounding terrain. There was the matter of the prisoner.

'Do we shoot the boy, or what?' he enquired easily.

'Why don't we string up the old couple an' take this one along as a hostage?' Prescott suggested.

Jake seemed surprised at the suggestion, but Meldrum, by his reaction, appeared to approve. Slim knew that Doc did not get worked up over nothing, and he, too, wanted to be off.

Between them they dropped a loop

over the necks of Skinney and Martha and hoisted them sufficiently high that anyone first approaching the oak behind the buildings would get the impression that they had died by the rope.

'If you're in a hurry, we ought to fire the buildin',' Jake suggested.

'I figure we won't wait that long,' Meldrum returned. He did not like the inference that they were in a great hurry, but he did not say anything about it. Jake was quick to fall in with their plans, and he mounted the pinto after tightening the saddle and rode off to the place where they had left their horses with poor Zack banging along behind.

The marauders left as quietly as they had arrived. Privately, each man wished he was back with the main party rather than taking the risks which they had assumed.

* * *

Red Storme moved in on Todd property less than half an hour later.

He whistled in a way peculiar to him, and was surprised when no one appeared to answer him. His sorrel took him in close, and he did not dismount until he was in the presence of the two dangling corpses which swayed with the tree bough in the gentle breeze. Although shocked, he was then all action, leaping to the ground and running to free the bodies in case there was any life left in them.

He was quick to discover how they had died, and the knife wound in Martha's breast reminded him of poor Paul Vance's silent despatch. Red's neck began to prickle. He hefted his Colt and began to prowl the buildings, but all he found was the limp form of Vance which had been overlooked when the other two were trussed up.

Red decided that the intruders must have been a trifle worried to forget to string up Vance. He also thought that they had not left very long ago. He called out up the meadow, in case Zack was still up there. Although he raised his voice, there was no reply. He then tried calling the name of the youngest member of the Todd household with as little success.

Red was as wise as Paul had been about Skinny's simple desires after death. He wanted to be buried under the oak which his enemies had used to string him up. Red fetched a spade out of the shed and went to work with it, digging a grave. He was at two-thirds of the necessary depth when a small figure started to come towards him from the land to the north.

As the digger paused to mop himself, he became aware of a young haunted face looking down at him. Red's eyes went to the two still forms, now covered by blankets.

'Why, Little Abe, how long have you been there?'

'Jest, jest a short time, Red, but I've been close for a long time. I — I saw what they did to Martha an' Skinny — an' Zack as well!'

'I'm real sorry you had to see it, Abe, an' you must be feelin' pretty awful, but there's things us survivors have to do. Will you help me?'

Little Abe was a dark, thin-featured lad of nine, given to the reading of books and other elementary forms of learning. He nodded eagerly, though his green eyes were bright with unshed tears and his fingers trembled.

'All right, then. Go put the pot on the stove, an' when you've done it, come out an' keep watch. You'll have to tell me a little about what's been goin' on, or else we won't know what to do about it. You understand?'

Abe's head was very clear. He carried out Red's instructions to the letter, and he had brought the sandy-haired man up to date, almost, by the time Skinny and Martha were laid in the grave, side by side.

'Why don't you put Paul Vance close to them, Red? It won't be very nice for him over at his place if it's been burned down!'

Red followed out this suggestion. He also questioned Abe, rather belatedly, about Zack, and got a shock when he heard how the older boy had been taken away alive. This knowledge made Red want to be on the move again without delay. He advised Abe to get a bundle of his clothes, enough to last him for a few days.

As soon as the boy was ready, they collected the mare from another meadow and set off for the Lazy K. This destination was reached without incident, and Tollman and his helpers were wised up as to what had transpired at the Todd home. Abe seemed quite content to stay with the Tollmans, and Red was glad that he had no ambitions to ride with the posse.

It was some hours later when Red finally caught up with the sheriff's party and learned how they had been harrying the main body of the invaders in an attempt to keep them from openly robbing and killing along the creek. They had been of the opinion that they had succeeded until Red came along and told them of the setback to the Todds.

All parties were disturbed about the abduction of Zack, too, but there seemed to be nothing they could do about it until the posse's numbers were boosted by settlers who were prepared to go over to the offensive. During that evening, Verleigh's party occupied a fine defensive position, and it was not until an hour after daylight that Grant discovered the enemy had flitted on during the night and recrossed the water.

12

Jim Storme partook of a good breakfast before leaving Fort Lerwick. He also took his leave of Captain Robb and Lieutenant Radwell with a good grace, and left them wondering why he was in such a pleasant frame of mind when he had apparently failed in his objective.

Sergeant Smith could have told them why, but he had little time for the inexperienced lieutenant or the domineering captain who was years behind for promotion to major. Smith's information was accurate as to the whereabouts of the hunting party, and Jim followed it out with due care.

As he threaded his lone way towards the north, Jim had much to think about. He knew that the sheriff and Bart were very keen to drive out the stockmen's mercenaries, but he wondered how many more of the small men would have to suffer before those who sought to bend the law were made to toe the line, and answer for their unjustified attacks upon the lesser men.

He felt sure that Red would survive, and probably Vance, too, although the rancher had been in far worse shape than Red when he had last seen them. He wondered if his holding of the ranch had materially helped his brother and the rancher, and fell to thinking about the future, and — in particular — his own task which Grant had thought to be a fruitless one.

Smith had explained how Major Brentford and George Thompson, the state governor, were close friends. He also mentioned how ill the governor had been, and how pleased the Major was when the state's head man came along and pronounced himself fit enough to indulge in a day or two of game hunting up country from the fort. The hunting had been a feature of life for the two friends since Thompson was elected governor when Wyoming achieved statehood.

With the two friends were six picked troopers, who could be trusted with the life of such an important man. Also with the party was a trapper and guide named Will Carter, who was more interested in shooting at animals than humans.

Jim reflected that the Major must have been very concerned about his friend, otherwise he would not have insisted on a separate medical check by the fort's surgeon. The officer in question had reluctantly given his permission to the governor, and that was how the hunt had become possible.

Through the heat of the mid-morning hours, Jim dozed in the saddle. The claybank did not appear to be over-endowed with energy, but it managed to keep up a good turn of speed when he asked for it, and as it was a borrowed horse he could not expect more.

Towards eleven o'clock, the thoughts of a rest and a brew of coffee began to tantalise him. He came wide awake, and studied the terrain around him. He was moving through a defile between two promising stands of scrub pine at the time.

The highest point in the area was a small peak called Dog's Leg, to the east. The nearest place where the hunters might be located was beyond a low ridge at the far end of the defile. Jim thought of the long distance he had ridden, of the slim possibility of his achieving success; and the wants of his body made him give in and take a spell off.

He built a useful-sized fire and set his coffee pot on the top of it as soon as it started to throw out any heat. He was just arriving at the idea that he did not like Wyoming as a place. He hoped the small men would win out against the cattle barons, and hold on to their lands. He also had no idea of leaving the state until such time as Red and Bart had the same idea. All the same, it was not the sort of place where he wanted to stay.

Texas now seemed a whole lot more attractive.

So did the enigmatic face of Maybell Dix. He recollected her long corn-coloured hair, the lithe shapely body which was as strong as a man's, and he wondered why the thoughts of Maybell had not drawn him with the same intensity in the past. He thought that men, perhaps, were as hard to understand as women.

And that thought carried him as far as the first mug of coffee.

A half-hour later, he moved on again, pushing resolutely for the landmark which was known on the few maps of the area as Sutler's Ridge. It was further off than he had thought, and he began to wonder what sort of a view there was from the top. He fed his imagination on the possibilities and laboured over the last few yards a good half-hour after midday.

The view was superb for anyone who had that sort of eye. It undulated into the distance in a lush green grid of small valleys and spiky ridges. His heart thumped as he saw the kind of activity he was looking for some two miles towards the north-west.

In the forefront of the riders, who were heading towards the ridge, were the two chief hunters, Major Brentford and Governor Thompson. Each man cut a fine figure, although there was every reason to believe that one of them was much fitter than the other.

Brentford sat a long-legged roan which appeared to eat up the distance with the length of its strides. He was a stiff-built man with a short black bristling moustache and brows. He rode with his body held well forward, and a certain intentness showed itself in the detail magnified by Jim's glass.

Governor Thompson was more than ten years older. He was in his middle sixties to be exact. He was taller than his friend and upwards of forty pounds above his best weight. It was obvious that he was in bad condition because his lungs were labouring due to the prolonged ride, and he kept blowing out the flecked walrus moustache which adorned his thick upper lip. He had on a magnificent white stetson, and he surveyed the world, human and animal, through a businesslike pair of metal rimmed spectacles.

Will Carter, the trapper and guide, could be picked out by his nondescript clothing. Will was a man in his middle forties who habitually wore stained trail garb. He was the only man connected with Fort Lerwick who could dress entirely as he liked. He had a permanent sun squint, and two days' growth of greying stubble fringed his leathery face and chin.

Will was riding with his drooping grey vest flapping, and seeking by every call and gesture to ensure that some animal not in sight kept between himself and the two keen hunters. Further back than the leaders, the six troopers who acted as guard were well strung out. They knew better than to forge ahead and deprive the Major and his important friend of the joy derived from the kill. Some of the general excitement communicated itself to Jim as he perceived the quarry for the first time. It was a huge bull moose with antlers spreading wider than those of any similar creature he had previously known.

It went forward from one small swale to another, occasionally pausing to take stock of the humans mounted on quadrupeds at his back. The noises it uttered would have put fear into most North American animals, but the horses came on apace, goaded by their keen masters to give their very best.

The moose seemed to sense that Will Carter was really the greatest menace. It covered a course which kept him almost a quarter of a mile away, and try as he might he could not lessen the distance. Brentford and Thompson, both of whom were better mounted, also tried hard without appreciably lessening the distance.

But they could afford to wait. From

time to time, Brentford wondered if his friend was over-straining himself, but George Thompson, in spite of his bulk and the heat of the day, showed no signs of wilting. The moose made two tentative moves to run along the foot of Sutler's Ridge, but the outriders fired off their weapons and in a short space of time it knew that it would have to fight what might be its last battle on the steeper slope.

Up it went, starting the climb with a big leap which was thrilling to the eye.

Jim watched their progress, as they laboured along behind the superb animal. He began to get less pleasure out of watching. Why should they be allowed to enjoy themselves in this boisterous fashion while the civilian population of the county was suffering through lack of support?

He began to entertain an idea which was at first rather shocking, inasmuch as it meant seriously interfering with the sport of the hunters. Dare he indulge his desire to influence them, or must he wait until the day's hunting was over and then hope for a kindly reception?

He thought about the way he had been received in the fort, and that decided him. If he could get their attention by a bit of chicanery, he would do so, and to the devil with the consequences! Bart and Sheriff Grant were striving with might and main, why shouldn't he?

In any case, if Major Brentford was at all like the character Sergeant Smith had given him, he would understand, in the long run.

Jim dismounted. He loosened his mount's cinch straps and led it a little further down the slope by which he had climbed. When its hooves were not clipping the loose stones in the earth's surface he was able to hear sounds of the hunt. He had little doubt that the quarry was moving steadily nearer the ridge, and that it would cross over on to the nearer side unless it was shot before then.

Smiling rather grimly to himself, Jim pulled out his Winchester and gave it his best attention. It was in perfect working order in spite of the rough treatment it had received during the fire at Vance's. He loaded it and checked it, and cradled it under his arm.

Some of his excitement communicated itself to the claybank, which by that time had grown quite used to him. It allowed itself to be led another fifty yards down the slope and tethered to a spiked shrub.

Jim fondled its neck and nose and promised that he would be back in a short time. He found himself wondering how many men in the West had left their mounts with similar thoughts and never lived to fork their saddles again. At least, he thought, what he intended to do would not endanger his own life. But who could tell?

He chose his position and lined up the Winchester on the part of the ridge where he expected the moose to first show itself. The time passed relatively quickly until it appeared. One minute the ridge was clear and the next the huge animal was standing with one pair of feet thrust over it, its magnificent antlers swaying slightly, and its body heaving with the continued effort.

Within seconds, it scented the cropping claybank. It swerved, as it began its downward run, so as to go further away from the horse and the marksman who had planted himself near it. Three huge leaps brought it well down from the crest. Two minutes later, Will Carter's labouring white horse popped into view with its grey mane tossing and its jaw dripping flecks of foam.

Will checked it and hurriedly glanced behind him. He, too, was tiring of the chase. He would have bowled over the moose at this juncture, had he been hunting simply for his own pleasure. The white horse side-footed. Will dismounted and tipped water into his hat. He was back in the saddle, having slaked the animal's thirst before the governor's smoke grey stallion hove into view a few yards ahead of Brentford's leggy roan.

'There he goes, Major!' Carter yelled hoarsely. He sucked in breath, wondering what the officer would do at this stage.

'Haul up, George, this is your chance,' Brentford bellowed.

Jim chuckled to himself. He could not afford to wait any longer. He panned the muzzle of his Winchester as the moose gathered itself for another huge leap, and squeezed the trigger. The bullet was well aimed. It homed on a vital spot and stopped the struggling animal at the very outset of its jump. Back it sagged on its haunches, and slowly toppled over, giving its last stricken call as its vitality went back on it.

Jim stood up, having done his dastardly work. He hurried over to the claybank, tightened the saddle and leapt on to its back while Governor Thompson was giving a brilliant imitation of a man who is thunder-struck. Carter yelled out in concern, and Brentford echoed him in consummate anger.

As the claybank started down the slope, Jim gave a gesture of derision and set his stetson more firmly on his head. This was the time when his plan ought to develop, if it was ever going to. If they didn't do what he expected, then he had spoiled his chance of an orthodox hearing later in the day.

Brentford fired a shot over Jim's head as first one, and then another of the escorting troopers came into view on the skyline. Soon they were all there, and every man knew that Brentford wanted the man captured who had ruined the governor's sport by shooting his quarry.

Jim sighed with a kind of relief as the enlisted men came down the slope after him. The claybank was tired, but the pursuing horses had been ridden hard since an early hour, so the chase was an even one. The pursuers were puzzled, not knowing that the man they pursued had a definite aim in view.

Down and down he went, then on, across the defile, and finally up the more tortuous western slope of Dog's Leg peak. From time to time, Brentford renewed his orders to overtake the man. The troopers struggled on, wondering how an ordinary day's hunting could have turned out like this, and where it would end.

Will Carter, urged along with the other men, began to go to the front. Jim was a little over a thousand feet above sea level when the claybank began to show signs of suffering. Instead of looking for a way to go progressively higher, he turned its head towards a southern shoulder, and once he was over that he had no inclination to go further.

He dismounted, fumbled out his glass and trained it on a distant happening well to the east. Carter was the first to come up with him. The guide turned a gun and an unwinking eye on him, while the others, toiling along behind him, gradually overhauled them.

Jim yawned. He continued to use his glass, but made a point of keeping his hands away from his weapons. Major Brentford was the fourth to arrive, after the guide. He had to wait for fully two minutes to get back sufficient breath to demand an explanation.

'Afternoon, Major,' Jim returned, with a grin. 'I wanted to see you personally, you an' the governor, about what's goin' on down there!'

Brentford dismounted and took the spy-glass from him as though it was red hot. Through it he saw a distant fire. The invaders had put another homestead to the torch. Brentford whistled and gave Jim another close look.

Jim went on: 'I rode all the way to Fort Lerwick to try an' get help for the civilian population who are bein' hounded and shot to death by an infamous bunch of hired mercenaries put into this state by the more ruthless of the big stock growers. They are backed up in their killin' by the indifference of an actin' governor an' an actin' C.O. who thinks it's all legal an' above board, an' maybe slightly funny. This was the only way I could get to you quickly. I'm sorry I spoiled the governor's sport, but I'll wager he'll understand.'

'How can he apologise for spoilin' my sport, an' why should I understand?'

The portly Thompson hove into view, having led his mount for the last few yards. Brentford started to fill him in on what Jim had said. Jim took over while the others rested. He talked with a burning conviction which had the troopers and Carter full of admiration.

In ten minutes he had said all that an ordinary man could say about such a situation, and given all the detail he could. Three times he stopped, and three times he anticipated the questions before they crossed the lips of the questioners.

The governor and the fort commander were left quite calm, although they were bathed in perspiration. Jim, however, was anything but calm.

He announced his intention of

heading back straight towards the troubled territory without waiting to know the outcome of the two important men's deliberations.

'Do I have your permission to leave, Major?' he asked formally.

'I don't have the powers to hold you, young man,' Brentford replied.

'But you do have other powers, an' the governor has more, if he'll use them before it's too late for hundreds of people!'

This was Jim's parting shot. He mounted the claybank, which a trooper held for him, and within fifteen minutes only the top of his hat, and occasionally his hunched shoulders, were still in sight. He left behind him a very thoughtful group of men, every one of which knew that something would have to be done about his intelligence and his demands.

Governor Thompson kept tugging at his walrus moustache and looking thoroughly down in the mouth. He knew that this hunt in his convalescence was at an end.

13

Verleigh and his invasion force first had the idea of using small splinter groups to keep the dwellers in the local territory on the hop, but the same strategy was soon adopted by Sheriff Grant and his fellow riders.

Unfortunately, however, Grant's smaller groups often arrived at isolated settlements after the damage was done. Two small shacks with little more than a meadow and a few head of cattle were shot up and burned on successive days, and thus Grant, who still had the responsibility for defence with no signs of assistance, had to change his plans.

It became obvious that the invaders had their spies as well as the settlers. At night camps, crawling men studied the disposition of the posse and carried away their valuable information to the other side. Sniping at night scared some of the men with large families.

The fighting and stalking went on, and some of the posse riders were on the point of asking permission to ride for their homes when Grant arose at an early hour one morning and drew aside Bart and Red.

'Boys, I don't think I like the way things are goin' any more than the members of the posse. The hombres who might have backed us up have stayed on the defensive behind their barricades, an' who can blame them? We have no reason to think that the numbers of the invaders are growin' but they're still doin' a whole lot of damage, though.

'I've been thinkin'. How would it be if the three of us broke away from the rest of the posse an' allowed it to become known that we have left them?'

Bart chewed on a stalk of grass, while Red mashed his hat brim with long sinewy fingers. 'But wouldn't this draw a whole lot more trouble towards the three of us?' the redhead queried.

'Sure,' Bart put in, 'that's what Amos is after. He knows the invaders are keen to knock out the peace officers. They think the defenders will be demoralised if that happens. It'll certainly take the heat off the posse men if we three break off an' leave them.'

All three men hunkered down out of earshot of the bustling camp. 'Of course, I know it's askin' rather a lot of you two,' the sheriff went on, 'but I figured you were both pretty well involved, in any case.'

'You were darned right to figure it that way, Amos,' Red answered quickly. 'Only in my case, I can't rightly rest until Jim comes back. Maybe if he got back fairly soon the four of us could team up an' lead Verleigh's best guns a dance?'

Grant chuckled. 'I figured you'd be thinkin' along those lines. I guess I'd feel the same way myself, if Jim was *my* brother. I'll put it to the other men. We three can then leave. An' as far as I'm concerned you, Red, can go lookin' for

Jim on your own, if you want to.'

Bart and Red agreed to this plan. After the breakfast, they noticed how quick Hank Norton was to seize the opportunity of taking charge of the main group, and hoped that nothing would happen to the men doomed to take his orders.

Grant concluded his talk by pointing out that the posse's chief function was to keep the main body of the invaders on the move until such time as the struggle materially altered.

'But what if it don't materially alter, Sheriff?' one doubtful posse man asked.

The question troubled the peace officer, but he screwed himself up to answer it. 'Tell me, mister, can you see this war goin' on indefinitely?'

The questioner shrugged rather than answered, and presently the key trio of riders moved away from the rest, who turned their attention to Hank Norton. He was strutting around the breakfast fire in a small circle. His eyes were on the ground. He looked to some like a mesmerised hen.

★   ★   ★

Red left the two peace officers within the hour. Using all he knew about the local terrain he pushed his sorrel along a course a few points north of westward, and wondered what his chances were of locating Jim in the vastness of the open country between the Sweetwater river to the south, Fort Lerwick in the west, and Sweetwater City to the north-east.

He began to see that he had set himself quite a task. Jim might approach the troubled area almost anywhere along a front of five to ten miles. Furthermore, in going off on his own, Red had seriously depleted Sheriff Grant's little force. In fact, he had cut it down by one-third, from three men to two. And Bart McGivern was his first cousin into the bargain. Red's bouts of conscience became more frequent. And yet, he felt that the pull of the blood could be forgiven, inasmuch as Jim was the only other Storme in any way close to him.

Red made his halts for rest and refreshment unreasonably short. He drove the sorrel and himself without pity, and the afternoon was far advanced when he changed the slant of his self-criticism, and decided that he was quite steadily lowering his powers of resistance, in the event that he should be attacked from cover.

With a sigh, he eased the pace of the sweating sorrel, and leaned forward to fondle its white blaze. He began to think that Wyoming state, and particularly Jackson County, was doing things to him; things which he did not really have to suffer. He, in his turn, began to think about Texas.

About an hour later, when he was thinking of stopping for a long halt, he found his way barred by a wide, but placid creek. He reined in and looked down on its smooth surface. It was like a mirror. With no difficulty at all, he could visualise the still forms of Skinny and Martha Todd, and the stiff features of Paul Vance, set in death.

A cold chill of horror ran down his spine. He blinked his eyes, hoping to shut such shocking memories out of his mind. The creek waters seemed to repel him. He decided that if he did not cross the water without delay, he would find himself inventing reasons why he should not cross at all.

Becoming brusque again, he stopped the sorrel drinking. He backed the animal out of the water and slackened off the saddle. His own boots came off, and then he was ready. He began the crossing with his feet held high to keep them dry. Just as he entered, he began to entertain for the first time the feeling that he was not entirely alone. It was a feeling he had learned to trust. He found himself glancing back over his shoulder and seeing nothing.

It was natural that he should look to his back, after the events of recent times. The sorrel, however, was ahead of him in locating the next human. A lolling figure, actually sleeping in the saddle, continued to come down the opposite bank of the creek from the north, the walking claybank having run out of land and simply turned its steps along the bank.

Seeing the drooping figure for the first time, Red did not believe his eyes. He put down what he saw to hallucinations. But soon he gave up screwing his eyes and decided that luck was on the side of the Stormes, for once.

He called: 'Hey, Jim, will you rouse up an' tell me if you're all right?'

Jim, for it was he, straightened up rather hastily and had his Winchester held across his body before his eyes told him that he was in the presence of his brother.

'You lookin' for me, Red?'

'That's about the size of things, brother!'

Red was still ten yards from the bank

when Jim called the obvious question.

'Vance is dead. He was found by a prowler while in the grip of a fever. I was on the run for a while, then I traced Paul to Skinny Todd's place. Unfortunately, Skinny and his wife had both been killed as well. I buried all three at the Todd homestead. An' what's your news, Jim? Did you have any luck when you made contact with the military?'

They came together, and the sorrel shook creek water over the two humans and the hard-ridden claybank. Jim mopped himself with his bandanna. He was scowling. His green eyes looked troubled. Across his forehead, the ventilated hat with the snake band had made a red mark. His chin wore a fringe of fair stubble. He would not have wanted Maybell Dix to see him in that state.

'It's hard to say about my mission, Red. Although I did contact the proper C.O. of the fort, an' the state governor who was out huntin' with him. They were impressed with what I had to say, but officials work slowly. I'd say it'll take a long time before we can count on the military to back us up.'

'What do you say if we make camp right here, an' rest up until dawn?' Red suggested.

Jim at once agreed. They began to strip off their saddles, talking steadily about recent happenings as they did so.

★　★　★

At eight o'clock the following morning they were back on the other side of the creek and riding their rested horses at a steady pace in a direction which ought to take them towards Sheriff Grant and Deputy McGivern with the minimum delay.

Jim remarked: 'Red, if anythin' happens to Bart before we get to him, how will that affect us?'

'I guess we'd soldier on for a bit, seein' as he was a chief deputy. Help out the sheriff, I mean. Do you see things that way?'

Jim nodded without enthusiasm.

There was still a silence between them when they became aware of another rider about to cut across their trail. Their own route lay in a south-easterly direction, whereas that of the other rider was coming from the north-east. They checked their pace, and presently he came upon them as they waited under the huge spread of a cottonwood. The Texan brothers had become extremely cautious in the last day or two. They contented themselves by simply nodding when the stranger hauled back on his reins and beamed at them rather uncertainly.

He was riding a roan gelding with a low barrel. It appeared to have started its journey for that day at an earlier hour than they had, or else it had been ridden quite hard. He was a man of about forty, with short, jet black hair, full-faced and with troubled grey pouched eyes. An imposing round black hat with a high crown topped his head making him look taller than his modest height.

'Howdy, fellows, I'm Jonathan Saddler by name. Goin' on an errand. Lookin' for the sheriff, as a matter of fact. You wouldn't have seen him in the last few hours, would you?'

'What did you want the sheriff for, Mister Saddler?' Red asked.

Saddler looked them over very carefully and seemed very reluctant to explain his predicament. Eventually, something in Jim's expression prompted him to try.

'I don't rightly know if you gents are strangers in these parts. Comin' from the direction you were movin' in you might be. In that case, you maybe wouldn't know Jackson County has certain troubles at the moment. I was sent to fetch the sheriff on account of certain prisoners he'd dearly like to have under lock an' key, you see!'

'Where are these prisoners?' Jim questioned.

'Well, if you're strangers, you won't be all that wiser if I tell, but the place is called Sangro's Mine.'

Red nudged Jim with his knee. He cleared his throat at the same time. 'Sangro's Mine is known to me, an' I'm no stranger to the district, Saddler. How come I don't know you?'

Saddler licked his lips. He seemed to find it hard to explain.

'Well, if you know Sangro's Mine, you'll know one or two other men since Sangro have tried to take the ore out of it. I'm the latest. I didn't figure to show myself near the towns until I'd found somethin' to shout about. Seems like a lame excuse, I know.

'Anyways, while I was out doin' a bit of huntin' two riders from a homestead were usin' my shack. They were sleepin' in the loft when three men came along an' kind of took over the place without seein' them. My guests came out in the night an' showed them the business end of their weapons. That's how these hombres was caught, see!'

'Describe them,' Jim prompted.

'Well, I'm a-wonderin' now what sort

of fellows you are, if you know these prisoners by their description.' Red snorted at this observation, and Saddler resumed rather hastily. 'One of them is a tall pale man with a pitted face. Another has a broken nose. The oldest one wears a fancy vest an' a nicely cut coat. Might have been a gambler at one time.'

'Those are the men we're interested in,' Jim replied excitedly. He turned his attention to Red. 'He's jest described Slim Meldrum, Dixie Bracknell an' Doc Prescott, the jaspers who figured at Vance's place!'

Red became suddenly keen. 'In that case, Saddler, we'll be glad to ride with you an' see those prisoners into the sheriff's hands. I'm Red Storme from Vance's place. McGivern, the chief deputy, is our cousin.'

Saddler appeared to almost sag with relief. He insisted on handing over two small cigars to the brothers, and chattered away about the difficulty of locating the ore in and around Sangro's

Mine. They stopped for a rest a little after one in the afternoon, and finally worked their way up the tortuous hillside to the location of Sangro's cabin about six in the evening.

On the last slope, Saddler's gelding began to blow rather badly. The messenger dropped slowly further behind while the brothers continued to make steady progress. They talked of how the capture of the Meldrum trio would alter the outcome of the small-scale war, and at times gave mildly optimistic views on the possible actions of Governor Thompson and Major Brentford.

The climbing path began to level out. The Sangro cabin was some three hundred yards along a patch of reasonably level ground, located under the seamed cliff where the original miner had prowled the caves in search of his fortune. There was no light in the cabin, and no welcoming filter of smoke came from the roof, either.

'Funny how easy wealth will draw men, even when others have failed miserably at the same spot,' Red remarked, as they cut down on the shrinking distance to the dwelling. 'Miners must have covered every inch of three caves at the back of the shack. An' what have they to show for it? Nothin' I guess.'

One of the miners had built a shed out of uneven lengths of timber. Another had taken a pair of rails into one of the caves. They were still in the same place, rusting, with a disused truck on them directly to one side of the shack.

'Anythin' wrong?' Red muttered, his eyes fixed on the distant darkened windows.

'I don't reckon so. Except that Saddler must be quite an observant fellow. He impressed me with the way he reeled off those descriptions.'

'But you could have done the same,' Red argued.

'Of course I could, but I'd ridden with them, hadn't I?'

They covered another fifty yards in

silence. Jim felt he had said something rather signficant, and yet he could not think why. He began to get a feeling of uneasiness. Glancing sideways, he saw that Red was experiencing the same. About a hundred yards separated them from the Sangro shack. The path to it was quite well marked. It split into two at eighty yards, one part going directly to the shack and the other path on the right going off down the side of the hill, under the overhanging cliff.

Jim said: 'What — ?' He hesitated.

'Over there, an' move pretty darned quick!' Red insisted.

He kneed the claybank to get it started and followed up with the sorrel which developed quite a long stride within ten yards. Side by side they almost flew towards the side track. A rifle opened up from the doorway. Red's bandanna was singed. A bullet tweaked Jim's belt and another hit his saddle cantle.

And then they were over the start of the track and dipping into the shelter of the intervening soil and rock. Someone in the building called an order in a hoarse voice. Another voice, markedly high-pitched, cursed them. There was a rush of feet, but by the time the marksmen reached the top of the secondary track, the fugitives were beyond maximum range.

They kept low over their horses' necks for some time after that.

When they had straightened up, Jim said: 'That Saddler wasn't with the mercenaries at the beginnin' but he sure knew Meldrum an' his buddies for the wrong sort of reasons. Quite an ingenious ambush, that was!'

'If Saddler crosses our path again, I'll salivate him without warnin',' Red promised.

It was almost nightfall when they spotted the flames of a fire. They had stumbled upon Grant and McGivern again. The sheriff seemed pleased to have them back until he heard the details of the Sangro ambush. After that, he insisted on a sharp watch being kept through the night.

14

The most recent experience of the Storme brothers put Sheriff Grant more on his mettle than ever before. He realised that his friends had survived an ambush which was most likely prepared for him and his deputy, if they could have been located easily.

The quartette broke camp at an early hour and picked up a course calculated to bring them near to the men at Sangro's cabin. The route was carefully thought out and would have brought about the clash they wanted, except that Meldrum had insisted on his followers leaving the hillside cabin the previous evening.

Even then, the sheriff's party succeeded in finding their sign, and getting on their track a useful distance to the rear. Grant had learned his tracking at an early age. He had acquired a distinct advantage by tagging on behind the killers. He did not intend to lose it. Wherever they were going, they had a destination in view. Probably they would go towards Captain Verleigh himself, and Milton Dodge, too, if he was still with the mercenaries.

Since the peace officers had left the posse, they had heard little to suggest where Norton had taken the riders. This continued to puzzle Amos Grant, as he and his fellow riders followed hard and came to the conclusion they were heading for Sweetwater Creek. The Creek, a northern tributary of the Sweetwater river, irrigated to some extent the remote country between the fort and the county seat.

About eleven in the morning, the pursuers lost touch but Grant was far from downhearted. He felt sure that they would regain contact when the quarry got as far as the creek. His optimism spread to Bart and for the time, the Stormes were willing to go along with anything Grant decided.

Five minutes after noon, they came out of timber on high ground overlooking the distant creek, and seeing a sight which amply repaid the sheriff's confidence.

There were riders on either side of the creek. On the near side, Meldrum and company had just rejoined Verleigh, Dodge and their headquarters riders. On the far side, some ten riders had just ridden downstream to emerge on the bank opposite the others. The talk between Meldrum and the Captain was cut short, as the spy-glasses showed.

The men waving from the further bank appeared to be in high spirits. Grant thought it probably meant they had eluded Norton and the posse. The sheriff blinked as something shone in his eyes; something at a greater distance. He made an adjustment to his spy-glass and held his breath. What he had glimpsed was too good to be true. He kept what he saw to himself.

The other three, aware of a change in

his outlook, wondered what was troubling him. First one glass was pointed in a new direction, then the others followed. Their ears were treated to the unexpected sound of a bugle. A great crescent of timber about seventy yards from the water's edge suddenly blossomed horses and men.

The riders were uniformed and smart. An officer pointed his naked sword and shouted an order which did not carry on account of the distance. The attack developed, however, with no sort of delay. Every rider fired his carbine at the loosely grouped mercenaries, and then broke into a charge.

The invaders milled about as if they could not credit this sudden onslaught. One of the horses sidefooted on the bank, lost its footing and deposited its rider into the waters of the creek. More bullets flew, each way at this stage. The charging riders converged upon the mercenaries. One trooper sailed out of his saddle as a bullet hit him. Another clawed his saddle leather and slipped to the ground with a stubborn show of reluctance.

A horse fell. As its mercenary master scrambled around on the ground, two of his fellows parted from leather and lay still around him. Others were wounded. The air was full of shrill cries and oaths. Those who had remained unscathed hurriedly launched their horses into the creek and crouched low.

The first of the advancing cavalry began to pull up on the bank.

A ragged volley from Verleigh's party taught them a new caution, but Dodge and the newly arrived trio were already heading away from the scene of the action towards the south. Major Brentford, leading the attacking force himself, called his men to dismount. From a kneeling position they poured successive shots into the men fording the water, and then into the other party on the opposite bank.

The swift encounter was at once exciting and relaxing to the four men who had waited so long for outside support. Grant found himself waving his hat and cheering like the other three. There was a lot of Texas fervour in their yahooing, but the mercenary army was far from yielding at that stage.

Verleigh, and the men with him, hastily withdrew into the cover of the nearest timber before going after those who had already moved off towards the south. Two men reached the bank, having escaped the soldiers' fusillade. Others were still struggling to do the same.

'It's time we were gettin' down there to fire a few angry shots!' Bart bellowed excitedly.

Grant patted his shoulder. 'I know how you're feelin', pardner, but I'm jest a little worried about my posse. Now the army is here it's time the posse was playin' a more prominent part in the action. Know what I mean?'

Jim nodded. 'Sure, sure, sheriff. We're with you on that, only our side is about to lose touch again if we don't move fairly quickly. Remember the cavalry is still on the other side of the creek!'

Faced by the three intent faces, Amos capitulated. By the time they were nearing the water, the cavalry had moved steadily further south, seeking a place where they could ford the creek in safety. Brentford was quite prepared to be out of touch for a short while before enjoining battle again.

Two dripping mercenaries separated and rode hard away from the quartette, but the main party of Verleigh's force managed to keep out of touch. Grant zigzagged; sometimes he kept close to the bank of the creek, and other times he operated a quarter of a mile away from it.

Occasionally they heard faint sounds, but the mercenaries stayed out of sight. Rests were infrequent. The horses began to wilt. Tempers became frayed. Eventually, they stopped for the night camp. Discussion was avoided. They took two-hour watches until daylight came again, and when a stray mule blundered among them and upset the coffee pot they took out their ill-temper upon it.

Grant, the oldest among them, spat coffee dregs into the fire and casually filled his lungs. He yelled: 'Methuselah!'

Red and Jim appeared to be startled, but Bart quickly recovered his good spirits.

'*Methuselah!* Can you hear me? This is Sheriff Grant callin' to you!'

This time there was a faint reply. Grant stalked away from the fire and followed the sound of the voice. They discovered an old man crouched in the fork of a tree about a hundred yards away. Methuselah had been old for as long as Grant could remember. He looked like a small imp up there with his wrinkled, spade-bearded face thrust through a hole in the middle of a dirty blanket, and a pinched stove-pipe hat jammed askew on his head.

'All right, all right, sheriff,' he protested, as the two peace officers glared up at him and asked him what he thought he was doing.

It was clear that the old man had made a colossal effort to get where he was, and that he had not the nerve to jump, or scramble down again. Bart stepped a little closer and caught him as he tentatively let go with one hand and lost his grip with the other.

This seemed at first like a comic interlude until they found what had speeded the old timer up the tree.

'They stopped real close, sheriff. Not all night, but long enough to make a scratch meal an' a few plans. That Captain fellow was almost off his head on account of the military attackin' his men back at the creek.'

'Did you find out where they planned to go, old man?' Grant asked, when the old fellow had warmed himself by the fire.

'There was a lot of arguin' goin' on, you understand, even after they'd broke camp. Mostly the shoutin' an' back-bitin' was between the Captain an' a fellow he called Dodge. But the

Captain knew what he wanted. He said he was damned if he was goin' to be put off because others were not up to the job. He was goin' to attack the Lazy K, as he had always intended! So now you know!'

'More trouble,' Amos commented. 'But that could be their last battle. I was right when I wanted to go after my posse. They're goin' to be needed, an' that real soon!'

'But perhaps the posse won't be anywhere near the Lazy K,' Jim conjectured.

'You're sayin' Tollman, an' the others ought to be told right away, before the posse, maybe.'

Grant looked around him. Red and Bart nodded. 'All right, then. I think you're right. You three Texans get yourselves over to the Lazy K, an' stay there, for the time bein'. I'll locate the posse on my own.'

Bart started to protest, but Amos cut him short, and fifteen minutes later the trio parted from the other two. All day the Texans pushed towards the creek where the Lazy K was located, adjacent to the Todd holdings. They kept a sharp lookout all the way, but saw no sign of Verleigh's party. That seemed to suggest a change of plan, or a less direct route.

Around six in the evening, they achieved their first distant sighting of the Tollman ranch. Their glasses showed them something rather disturbing. Bart was the one who first gave vent to his feelings.

'Will you look at that, boys? Upwards of a dozen grown men rippin' out the stakes they stuck in the ground to keep back the enemy!'

Red sighed. 'I suppose it's understandable, if they've heard the cavalry has entered the struggle on our side, but they shouldn't have acted so swiftly.'

'If we gallop all the way now we shan't get there in time to stop them rippin' the defences apart. It's lucky for them we met Methuselah an' came straight along to warn them,' Jim added.

He was thinking that the cavalry was some distance off, and out of touch with probable developments. And when the posse would arrive was anyone's guess.

15

They rode into Lazy K ground as a tight trio with Bart in the centre wearing his badge. By the time they arrived all the defensive stakes which had been planted around the front of the six ranch buildings had been pulled down. The wooden defences to the rear would have received the same treatment, except for the demolishers' need to slake their thirst. A dozen men had piled into Dick Tollman's kitchen to sample his wife's coffee, and thus the work had ceased for a time.

While Mrs Tollman and her daughter, Vera, poured out the coffee, Tollman, himself, and his son, Mathew, entertained a messenger; in fact, the man who had brought the tidings about the arrival of the troops and the invaders' setback by the creek.

Their horses were tethered along the

hitch rails under the front gallery of the house. Men and boys were coming and going. Several of them knew Red as Big Sandy, and they called out to him, knowing that he had had a tough time when Vance was killed.

Bart touched his hat to others. He, too, was known, because of his association with Amos Grant. Jim hung back. He was studying two well dug slit trenches in the yard in front of the house. One of them had been filled in, but the other was still workable. He glanced idly around the men and women, boys and girls, who had sought a sort of sanctuary inside the Lazy K defences, and wondered how they would react when the invaders came against the place full of venom and wickedness over earlier setbacks.

Suddenly his eyes strayed to the restless horses belonging to others. A memory primed his brain. Red and Bart were strolling up the front steps of the gallery, nodding to an old man who might have been Dick Tollman's father.

The low-barrelled roan gelding which had taken Jim's attention gnawed fretfully at a post.

Recollecting his brother's earlier narrow escapes, he started up the steps, brushed the other two aside, and stepped into the building ahead of the startled old man. Keeping his head down, he blinked hard to accustom himself to the inner gloom, and noticed two men seated in easy chairs on either side of the fireplace.

One of them seemed markedly still, while the other set aside a shot glass and grinned good-humouredly towards the door. Tollman was in his late forties; a round-faced man, barrel-chested and bald headed. A dark chin stubble hinted at the length of time since he last shaved. He scratched his hirsute chest through a checked shirt and waved a hand, as his son, Mathew, entered by another door.

'I don't know who you are, mister, but on this day of all days you're welcome!'

'Stand well away, Mister Tollman!'

Young Mathew, a stocky, ruddy-faced youth with a long nose, backed away when he saw the Colt leap into Jim's fist. Jonathan Saddler moved with the speed of a snake, but Jim was ahead of him by a second. Crockery and china ornaments clattered and rattled to the blast of guns.

Jim's first bullet ripped into the messenger's chest. Saddler's reply entered the lion skin at his feet. A second shot from Jim's Colt hit the cunning interloper in the head as he slipped to the floor.

There were several seconds of silence as the smoke and powder swirled around the room. Jim remained quite still in the position near the front door where he had gone into action. So did Mathew, his father having slumped back into his chair. A voice from the kitchen, slightly off-key, demanded to know what was going on.

Bart McGivern got into the room just ahead of Red. For a few seconds

Bart had his doubts about what Jim had done. Red spoke up.

'Jonathan Saddler, eh? I guess you must have seen his hoss, Jim.'

Between them, Bart and Red carried out the limp form and draped it on the front gallery. As there were children about, they covered it at once.

Jim said: 'Sorry to scare you like that in your own parlour, Mister Tollman. I don't suppose you knew you were harbourin' one of the enemy!'

Suddenly the rancher was furious. He threw his shot glass across the room and pointed a threatening finger. 'Mister, you'd better have a whole lot of good talk to back up what you jest did because that fellow never came in with the stockmen's army! He was bringin' good news! He said the cavalry had defeated the invaders at Sweetwater Creek! Now, is that right, or is it not?'

Red came in and saw how things were. 'Sure, the cavalry is in the district, an' they fired on an' scattered part of the stockmen's force. But you ain't safe yet, because the stockmen's army is headed this way. They aim to attack your ranch to make up for recent setbacks.'

Bart added: 'That's the way things are. It's a pity we couldn't get here sooner. Then the stakes could have been left in place.'

Tollman sent his wife a reassuring message and told his son to go out to the kitchen and fetch more coffee, but he was still far from pleased about recent events. Soon, he was pacing between the three tall Texans, and clearly full of misgivings.

'But what you boys are sayin' don't make sense! If the invaders have lost some of their men they'll be retreatin', on the run! They won't throw all their guns against a defended place like this!'

'It isn't defended like it was, Dick, an' they are past carin' what becomes of them, I should think! In any case, the Captain in charge of them is an opportunist. He might jest catch you when you were not ready.' Red sighed.

He could see that his words were not impressing Tollman. He added: 'Did you ever go along to see what they did to Vance's place?'

Tollman said he had been to Vance's place and he still was not convinced that his property, and the neighbours who had temporarily moved in on him, were in any danger. Someone knocked on the front window, and a moment later, in came Little Abe, Skinny Todd's boy.

He announced: 'Zack is back, an' he says the killers are comin' here.'

Zack hobbled in. While the women pushed through the men to attend his skinned wrists and ankles, he told how he had slipped away from the enemy, and how he had heard the Lazy K discussed, as had the old man, Methuselah. Zack's information did a deal of good, killing a lot of the hostile feeling kindled against Jim over the shooting of John Saddler.

* * *

When the trio of Texans arrived at the Lazy K, there remained some four hours of daylight. An hour before dusk, the garrison of the place had taken up defensive positions, and all the children and women were well out of sight. Tollman was still blatantly sceptical about an attack, and so were the other homesteaders helping with the defence.

The actions of the Stormes, however, and the chief deputy, made them stop passing scathing remarks and take the matter seriously.

Bart insisted that his cousins and he should man the one good slit trench in front of the house. No one argued with him over that. The small ranchers could hardly do so, seeing as how they did not believe an attack would come. Forty minutes of daylight remained when the first volley came out of the trees behind the house and alerted the defenders. After that, there was no more scoffing.

Rather belatedly, Bart left his trench and ran back to the house. 'My cousins have jest come up with a good suggestion. If they use a go-devil again, try the effects of a hosepipe on it.'

Tollman sniffed.

'You deserve to lose your house, you fool!' Bart yelled. 'Not long ago you wouldn't believe they'd come, an' we moved a killer from your own parlour! I wish we hadn't come here now!'

Bart ran back to the trench, already regretting his words.

As the sun's light faded from the west, the scattered attackers gradually converged on the front of the buildings, actually attacking up a slight slope. Eight riders came up close. Two of their number were shot and spilled to the ground by accurate shooting from the trench.

After that, the idea of a cavalry charge approach was shelved. A cart appeared, as in the attack on the Vance ranch, but this time there were no signs of its being used for the same purpose. Tollman, perhaps still over-confident, believed it would not be used because of the uphill slope to the buildings.

Although they were out of touch, the

trio in the trench hoped the same hopes. Anything in the explosive line, dropping short of the house, might speed them to the next world with little warning.

Red, Bart and Jim were kept busy. Soon their rifle barrels were hot to the touch. Their ammunition went down quite steadily, and became a source of anxiety. About an hour after the firing had begun, there was a short lull. This served to put everyone's nerves on edge.

The lull ended when two men lit torches and hurled them from a prone position against the house. The men in the trench fired only three rounds against these latest attackers, and it was rightly deduced that they had few more bullets to fire. The torches were only torches, and not explosives. The same was tried again.

This time Jim yelled for the others not to fire. 'They're tryin' us out. Why don't we go along with their ideas, an' maybe kid them we're out of ammunition?'

'It's a gamble, but it might do the defenders a lot of good,' Red replied.

'All right,' Bart agreed. 'If they actually make us fire our last we might still be able to crawl clear. Maybe they'll be friendlier to us at the house by now.'

A half-hour dragged by with all the spasmodic firing directed at the front of the buildings. Soon after that, there were sounds which indicated that horses were being moved. The optimists among the defenders thought perhaps that the attackers were withdrawing, but such was not the case. In fact, the main attack was imminent.

The sound of the cracking whip was the warning of what was happening. Up the slope came the cart, swaying at speed, and ghostly in the dark. Four good horses pulled it, and the man who held the reins was as hard to pick out as the men who hovered in the back, under the canvas awning.

Rifles began to pour bullets at the team, but still the whip held sway and the vehicle continued to approach. Jim began to feel distinctly uncomfortable. He could see on the faces of his brother and cousin similar doubts about the outcome of this clash.

'Do we fire on them, or not?' Bart queried.

'I say we hold back for as long as possible,' Jim suggested.

'An' we look out for anyone lobbin' a dynamite stick into the trench,' Red added.

At this reminder, all three began to perspire at the uncertainty. The cart came level with their position. Rifles were now firing against the house out of the back of it. One pair of wheels rocked as they moved over the filled-in trench. The other pair narrowly missed the end of the occupied one.

Jim distinctly heard the spluttering of a fuse. 'Here comes trouble!' he called.

They waited, tensed for anything. The stick of explosive was hurled out of the front of the attack wagon, but not at the trench. It landed on the threshold of the front door of the ranch, and there it spluttered, while several shoulder guns aimed at the door and the window beside it. A slim figure slipped out of the door, leapt for the spluttering fuse, and succeeded in standing on it. The flame went out. At the same time, the bullets sought and found the valiant one.

Young Zack Todd sank to the ground, having died heroically.

Seconds later, the hose, trained through the window, was aimed at the box of the cart. The prancing horses blocked some of the jet, but the rest got through, taking the hidden guns by surprise. Menaced by bullets and the jet of water, the attackers faltered. As the horses swerved to one side, the gunmen spilled out of the back, trying to regain their breath, and retain their sense of direction in the dark.

Jim breasted the rim of the trench. 'All right you men, hold it! You're covered! Drop your guns, an' raise your hands!'

'That's Storme's voice,' Bracknell complained.

Prescott added: 'Sure, I'd know it anywhere! What are we waitin' for? We know they're out of ammunition. Right now that trench sounds like a good place to be!'

Bullets hastily fired came towards the trench. Jim had shifted his position. The shoulder weapons of the trench defenders sounded off in unison. As fast as they could lever, the Texans fired. The hired guns were caught in the crossfire between trench and house.

Jim accounted for a man who afterwards turned out to be Bracknell. Red and Bart both claimed a hit on the corpse of Prescott. But that was later. The lethal display of bright gun muzzles continued for almost a minute. Inevitably, the trench defenders stopped firing first. They were also the first to hear the surrender cries.

'Hold it! *Hold it, will you?*'

No less than nine corpses were later found on the ground between the trench and the house. The man who cried out for quarter was Slim Meldrum, himself. Hovering near him was a familiar dark-skinned man, Arizona Jake. The latter had thrown away his deadly knife, and raised his hands as high as he could get them.

The Storme brothers stayed alert in the trench, while Bart clambered out and took charge of the two tricky prisoners.

The more distant firing became spasmodic. After another fifteen minutes it gave way to a lot of shouted orders which carried only indistinctly to the troubled defenders. Then came sounds from beyond the wooden pallisade at the rear.

A voice which was used to authority called: 'Hey, there, you men defendin' the Lazy K. This is a spokesman for the United States cavalry. On no account come away from the house in the near future. The army will be very busy, an' we shall take all men outside Lazy K territory to be enemies.'

The message was repeated and acknowledged.

The pursuit and routing of the remaining invaders was about to begin.

16

By dawn the forces of the invaders were vanquished.

Captain Verleigh, along with Milton Dodge and one or two other men, was pursued by the cavalry for several miles, and because of his superb white stallion there was a time when he might have slipped away and perhaps escaped.

Within an hour of dawn, however, Sheriff Grant and his posse met them almost head on. To give them their due, the stockmen's mercenaries were more alert. Because of their swift reaction, they were able to avoid swift annihilation and turn about. From that time forward, it became clear that further resistance, even flight, was impossible.

Verleigh surrendered his sword to Major Brentford, who was following up close, and that ended the affair.

* ★ ★

The delighted settlers who had camped at Tollman's place were quick to get back to their own property. For two or three days, the Stormes stayed on. Most of the time they were just resting, and occasionally they talked, and wondered when they could lure Bart away from the sheriff's office without letting down the sheriff himself.

When the invading prisoners were safely behind bars, a remarkable change came over many of the small ranchers and settlers. They clamoured for the ring-leaders to be hung, believing that if they went for trial smooth-tongued lawyers could get them off.

So strong and persistent were the demands of the people that Sheriff Grant feared that his cell block might be invaded at any time. The people who should have been backing him to the limit were his new enemies. He was considerably dismayed when moderate small men expressed the same strong views as the hotheads; namely, that the leaders of the invasion forces should die by the rope.

Eventually, he was so distressed that he made special arrangements to have Verleigh, Dodge, and several others removed by train to the lock-up of a neutral county further south.

Bart McGivern, who had announced his intention of leaving Wyoming for his native soil, undertook to take charge of the escort as his last job wearing a deputy sheriff's badge. Jim and Red were deputised to go along with him, and within a week of the debacle at the Lazy K, the prisoners were smuggled aboard a train, and hurriedly taken out of Jackson County.

A small detail of the cavalry sided them as far as Sweetwater depot. After that, prisoners and escort were on their own. And the notoriety of the accused had spread far and wide, and well beyond the borders of Grant's troubled territory.

Bart and his cousins found themselves examining every man who got on the train at the early stops. Inevitably, after a time, their vigilance waned. They were tired, and their tiredness had accumulated over a long period. All they wanted was a quiet trip to Texas, and here they were, still vitally involved in the outcome of the Wyoming settlers' struggles, long after everyone else had gone home.

Red and Bart dozed, while Jim kept awake. For perhaps the twentieth time, he studied the slumped forms of the six prisoners, and wondered whether they still had enough fire in their bellies to attempt an escape; or whether, in fact, some of their staunch allies in the stock growers' association might seek to spring them loose before they saw the inside of a court-house. At that time, they all looked thoroughly subdued. They were handcuffed in pairs. Slim Meldrum and Arizona Jake were linked. So were Verleigh and Dodge. The third pair were also hired guns. Archer was a slim, deadly man from Tennessee, and his partner was a swarthy fellow named Morden from Louisiana.

The journey had started before dawn. The advent of the sun had made them all sleepy.

Jim kept guard until around one o'clock. He was about to shake Bart when the locomotive began to slow down. He glanced out of the window and saw that they were in an isolated spot between towns. Red and Bart came awake at once. The prisoners did the same, but they stayed still and showed no particular interest.

Further back on the train, the conductor put his head out and looked forward.

The engineer called out: 'We're out of water, mister. Do you have any spare at the rear of the train?'

'Not enough to fill a boiler, anyways,' the incensed conductor yelled back.

The guards thought the situation had a slight smell to it. The train had other, ordinary passengers on it. It also had an express car, with a messenger and telegraph clerk in it. The Texans could almost read one another's thoughts. They were wondering how they would be affected if this was an ordinary hold-up of the express car, staged well away from people, between towns.

The carriages jerked to a halt. Bart remarked: 'I think we ought to look into this, jest in case there's anythin' special behind it.'

Dodge and Verleigh had guarded looks on their faces. Meldrum and Arizona Jake seemed mildly pleased. They were enjoying the discomfiture of their guards, but they did not appear to be excited enough to anticipate a dramatic rescue attempt.

'All right, let's try it,' Jim replied.

'We can't all go an' leave the prisoners,' Red protested. 'I tell you what. I'll go as far as the loco. Bart could take a look at the express car, if he felt like it.'

'An' that leaves me right back where I am, in this corner,' Jim grumbled.

He approved of the plan, however, and within seconds he was left with his restless prisoners.

* * *

There were no signs of undesirables approaching the train on either side of the track. Having satisfied themselves of this, Red and Bart cleared off on their errands. Red dropped to the ground and ran forward with his rifle held close, while Bart stalked through the various compartments with his restless eyes taking in the startled passengers.

Red swung up on to the footplate. 'You the engineer here, mister?'

An overweight, stooping individual with a drooping jowl and watery eyes admitted to being the engineer. His face lengthened when Red asked him how he could possibly let the loco run out of water at such a Godforsaken spot. He seemed short of words, and anxious for Red to get back to his seat.

The fireboy, however, a darting ferret-like man in a cap with an outsized peak, acted differently.

'Why don't you step aside, Joss, an' let the gent come up here? He could see for himself that what's happened aint' through any negligence of yours!'

Red peered past the engineer, who reluctantly drew back, as though to make way for him. Red never did get into the cab. Just as he made as if to swing himself up, the fireboy produced a long-barrelled revolver and shot him in the chest from less than a yard away.

Red frowned. His eyes rounded as he realised that he was dying. He slipped backwards, lost his grip, and fell to the side of the permanent way, mouthing the name of his brother. He managed to lift his head off the ground for two or three seconds, then his strength gave out. He settled back, still and dead.

Messenger and clerk heard the shot, and decided against opening their special carriage to the deputy in charge of the prisoners. They were suspicious.

Bart hovered outside their express car, wondering what he should do. Further back, Jim stuck his head out of a doorway and at once beheld the still figure of Red. His heart lurched as it had never done before.

The prisoners were only of secondary consideration now. He dropped to the lines and ran forward, shouting to Bart every few yards. Soon, he was on his knees beside the still figure of his older brother, and he knew the worst. Bart joined him there, and was almost as distressed.

The shaky sobbing of the engineer cut across their shock. They were told how the temporary fireboy, a stranger, had done the shooting and then disappeared. Leaving Red where he was, they went back and clambered aboard the train behind the express car. From there, they moved slowly through the compartments looking for a man whose face was known only to the engineer. Men quaked as they saw them, but when they approached the

252

carriage in which the prisoners were housed there was another shock awaiting them.

Several armed men in masks suddenly surrounded them. Some were dressed in riding clothes, but the majority wore derby hats and stores suits, and appeared to be among the passengers from Jackson County.

The leader, a man with a long nose and a nasal way of talking, urged them to get down out of the train to track level. Four masked men accompanied them and took their weapons, while another six hustled out the prisoners on the other side.

'If you're thinkin' or doin' what I think you're doin' I have to tell you you're breakin' the law!' Bart insisted hoarsely.

Jim told him to save his breath. By bending down, they were able to see the three handcuffed pairs of prisoners as they were lined up in front of the avenging guns. One swift volley was all that was needed. The condemned men had been so stunned by the swiftness of the happening that they had scarcely protested. Meldrum called out part of an oath, and Dodge began a high-pitched plea, but that was as far as they got.

An immediate attempt was made to get the deputies back on board. They refused until Red's body was lifted into their compartment. Five miles down the line, they were given the chance to leave, with their horses, and they took it.

No conversation passed between them as they jogged away from the railway line, with Red's limp body swinging on the back of his sorrel. In a slim virgin belt of scrub pine, they agreed upon a burial place. Their spades bit into the earth, side by side. While they worked, the train's whistle sounded. The loco moved off again. Neither of them showed the slightest interest about how the empty boiler had been filled earlier. When the grave was prepared, they withdrew a few yards and rolled a couple of smokes.

Jim said: 'Bart, this territory is not for the likes of us. Maybe we were wrong to respond in the way we did when our feet got itchy an' we moved north. Understand this, Texas may be ruined by bob-wire from the Panhandle to the Rio Grande, but after this here's one son who'll stay there, come what may!'

'We couldn't have known how things would turn out when we rode north, Jim,' Bart pointed out sympathetically.

'How about that little rat of a fireboy? Do you reckon the shootin' of Red was not intended, like the masked man said?'

'I reckon it might have been that way, Jim. In any case, those eyes we saw over the masks looked lethal enough to kill him for killin' when he shouldn't have. I wouldn't be surprised if he's dead when they reach the next station.'

Jim was long in answering. 'I'm glad you think it'll turn out that way, Bart. Because I'm the last of the Stormes, an' in other circumstances I ought to search the whole of the earth until Red's life is avenged. Right now, though, the idea of shootin' to kill makes my stomach turn over. I couldn't do it. Not even for Red. Is it bad when a man feels this way?'

Bart shook his head. He sounded extremely wise when he answered.

'Killin' is not natural. You've been too close to too much killin' for a long time. What you want is the fresh air of Texas, maybe the breeze offen the Gulf, an' a lot of cowpunchin'. Sometimes I think that cows are a whole lot cleaner in their ways than men.'

Bart waited until Jim was ready for the interment. They rose silently together, bareheaded and heavy with distress. Big men as they were, they were as gentle as women as they lowered the redhead into the pit. Between them, they improvised snatches of the burial service, and then repeated prayers which they had thought to be long forgotten.

Finally, they replaced the earth and fashioned a simple wooden cross which gave all the details necessary.

In the next town further south, Bart telegraphed a message to Sheriff Grant, explaining what had happened on the unfinished journey to the neutral county town. He took a copy of the message to the town marshal's office and left it there, along with his badge.

★   ★   ★

After that, they made steady progress towards the lone star state.

The white-blazed sorrel went along with them as a spare, with Red's saddle loosely fastened to its back. Jim used to stare at the trappings sometimes.

'Do you think if we get back home with an empty saddle, the folks won't have to ask for details, Bart?' he queried once.

'I think if they see it that way, they'll wait for you to tell them what you want them to know,' replied the ex-deputy.

He was hoping that the loss would be easier to bear by the time they reached the Panhandle.